FIVE
KNIVES

a novel by

D. F. BAILEY

COPYRIGHT NOTICE

Five Knives
Copyright © D. F. Bailey 2018: Registration #1145816
ISBN: 978-0-9950483-7-9
Published by Catchword Publishing
Edited by: Dave Henry

Acknowledgements — I am extremely grateful to Lawrence Russell and Rick Gibbs for reading the early versions of Five Knives. Their insights, wisdom and advice were invaluable to me as I worked through the final draft of the novel. — DFB

For more information about D. F. Bailey and to join his VIP Readers Club visit dfbailey.com.

One Reporter.

Three Dead.

Five Knives.

※

Inspired by true events

FIVE KNIVES

CHAPTER ONE

Will Finch saw the corpse less than a minute after he heard the horrible noise. He never imagined that death could sound so leaden. And yet, so wet. The punch of a heavy body splatting onto flat concrete. A splash punctuated by a gasp. Then a faint wheeze as the lungs released a final breath into the city night.

At first, he couldn't see the body. Four people stood on the sidewalk blocking his view. Their heads tipped down at an angle as they absorbed the catastrophe that sprawled next to their feet.

"What happened?" Finch pushed forward and stepped around the blonde girl. She held a hand to her mouth and let out a cry.

"I don't know." The boy next to her glanced at the building above them. "He fell," he offered with a stony expression.

Finch studied them a moment. Two couples in their midteens, white, vibrant, all well-bred and dressed for dinner at an upscale restaurant in nearby Jackson Square. Probably making

1

their way down to the Embarcadero where they could catch a street car or train back to their suburban homes. He checked his watch. 11:18. These kids were probably trying to beat their midnight curfews.

But now he observed the change coming over them. The reality seeping in. One by one, the cold hand of death caressed their faces and forced them to look again at the bloody pulp on the ground. *Turn and watch. This is what I can do.*

"Did you see him fall?" Finch studied their shocked expressions. Two girls and two boys, standing stock-still. They all shrugged and glanced away from the corpse. One of the boys lurched to the sidewalk curb and vomited into the gutter.

"Yeah. I did." The blonde rubbed a hand over her mouth, her trance now broken. "Just in the last second."

"Do you have a phone?"

"What?" She glanced at him for the first time. Her eyes swept over his face as if she were memorizing the features of his eyes, nose, mouth.

"To call 9-1-1."

Her look suggested some uncertainty. Then she rummaged through a small purse that hung from her shoulder by a chain strap.

"Here." She offered Finch her Nokia.

He made a mental note of her number on the flash screen, then placed the call. The dispatcher advised him that a response team would be by as soon as possible. Meanwhile, he should remain on the line and not leave the scene. As he waited, he leaned his buttocks on the door of a parked car, pressed his ear to the cellphone and stared at the building. He counted fourteen stories which rose above the Bank of America outlet on the corner of Stockton and Washington Streets. He tried to determine how many apartments had open windows. Maybe six. His eyes swept from room to room, scanned for fluttering curtains or someone above who might be peering back at him. Nothing.

Then he detected something unusual. Behind the curtains in an apartment on the eleventh floor a lamp clicked on, then off. On and off. As the pattern continued Finch tried to time the periods of each interval. Five seconds, seven, ten. Then the apartment blinked into darkness. And lit up again.

Finch made another calculation: the intermittent flashes came from the sixth window along the left side of the building. He guessed that each apartment had two windows facing the street. The third apartment in from the north side on the eleventh floor had one window open, one closed. The room behind the closed window was the source of the flashing light.

He took the phone from his ear and passed it to the blonde. "What's your name?

"Alice."

"Alice?"

"Winkler," she added.

"All right, Alice. My name's Will Finch. The 9-1-1 dispatch said someone should be here soon. They want you to stay here and stay on the line." He gave her a serious look. "Now I think I saw something up there, so I'm going to see what happened."

"Okay." She said this as if she were making a polite concession and then held the phone to her ear and nodded. She turned to her friends. Both were tending to the boy who'd lost his dinner.

Will walked along Washington Street past the bank and approached the glass doors that led into the apartment building. He tugged on the handles. Both doors were locked. He stepped to the curb and turned his attention back to Alice and her friends. Three pedestrians had come to their aid, and then an older couple coaxing a Shih Tzu on a leash paused to provide more support. Another minute passed, and Finch saw a couple approaching the building entrance from the interior elevator bay. He stepped up to the door. When it opened, he smiled at the two women strolling past him and said, "Thanks. I don't seem to have my key."

He rode the elevator alone up to the eleventh floor and wondered if he'd counted everything correctly. The car door opened onto a hallway illuminated by covered fluorescent ceiling lights. The carpets bore a floral pattern of braided roses that stretched from one end of the empty corridor to the other. As he eased toward the north side of the tower, he detected the flat odors of fried food. Years of fried chicken and beef dinners had added their heavy flavors to the stale air. He guessed that the building was about thirty years old. Perhaps it had once been an impressive residential tower, but years of wear and disrepair had tarnished its pedigree.

He stepped along the passageway counting off the numbers on the street-side apartments. 1110, 1108, 1106. He approached 1104, the third door from the end of the hallway. Like all the others, it was closed. He knocked once, twice — and again. Nothing. He pressed an ear to the wood panel. From the apartment's interior, he could make out a quiet mewling. The sound of a puppy whimpering? In the distance, he heard the wail of approaching sirens.

He hesitated for a moment and wondered what he was doing. What business is it of yours? Good question, he decided and made a bargain with himself. He would try the door handle, and if it were locked, he'd go back to the street and tell the emergency responders what he'd discovered. On the other hand, if the door were unlocked, he'd go in.

He turned the handle. The door opened.

※

He stepped onto the beige carpet and closed the door behind him. He paused a moment to assure himself that he was making the right move. Who could know? The apartment appeared to have a standard one-bedroom layout. To his right stood a galley kitchen with an eating nook that faced into the living room. On the left, a bathroom. Adjacent to the bathroom a closed door — which Finch assumed led into the bedroom.

Directly in front of him, he could see the living room window had been pulled open. The sheer drapes, drawn tight to the side window frames, lofted slightly in the breeze coming off the bay. Finch sniffed the air. It smelled fresh, full of life. He heard the emergency vehicles stop on the street as the blare from their sirens wound down. The whimpering noise he'd heard from the corridor was detectable again.

He walked to the open window and stood to the left of the window frame. From there he peered onto the street. Directly below him lay the corpse, which from eleven floors up, appeared to be little more than a sack of flattened pulp leaking a dark stream of blood that slipped toward the curb. A crowd of fifteen or twenty people made way for the ambulance crew. A fire truck pulled up behind the ambulance. One of the attendants approached Alice, who still held the phone to her ear. They began to talk and she slipped the phone into a pocket. Her friends moved to the corner across the street. One of the boys waved to her, a gesture to let her know they were still present, if not at her side.

The trucks left their flashers on alert. The silence surprised Finch, and for a moment he tried to grasp the conversation of the ambulance crew as they attended to the body. He could make out a few words, some standard commands, he guessed, but no complete sentences.

Then he heard the mewling again. He turned from the window and approached the bedroom door.

"Hello?" He tapped the door panel with a knuckle and said, "There's been an accident. I'm here to check on you."

The whimpering now turned into something more human. A gasp of surprise.

"What? See-See, is that you?" A woman's voice, rigid with fear.

Finch eased the door open. The bedroom was half the size of the living room. The curtains were pulled tight across the window. With her left hand, the woman clutched the bedpost opposite the door. Her left leg was poised on the floor as if she was about to stand. The right calf was curled under her thigh and resting on the bed. She wore a bra and panties. Nothing else. Her almond-blonde hair was disheveled. It appeared as if she'd just showered but hadn't had time to dry and brush her hair. From where he stood Will thought that she could be leaning on the post to support herself.

"Jeez. Who are you?"

Her question came out with another whimper. Finch felt confident she was the source of the cries he'd heard from the hall.

"Do you need some help?"

"Help?" A startled frown crossed her face, then a rising awareness that something had changed. "Get me that key," she demanded and shook her wrist against the bedpost. She flicked her free hand toward the bureau in the corner.

Finch now saw the handcuff that clamped her left wrist to the post. He moved to the bureau and examined a standard handcuff key that sat in a glass ashtray on top of the bureau. Will almost picked up the key, then thought again. He turned to face her.

"Who busted you?"

"Busted me?" A flash of panic gripped her face. "No one busted me. This is all a setup for some psycho with a rape fantasy."

A stick lamp stood on the bedside table next to her. He assumed that she'd been able to reach the light with her free hand.

"Was that you clicking the lamp on and off?"

"Yes, damn it!" Her panic shifted to exasperation. "Now get the key so we can both get out of here before it's too late." She tipped her head back toward the bureau.

"Before what?"

"Before we both get thrown out the fucking window!"

The panic in her voice sent a chill through him and he knew he had to take her seriously. At the same time, his doubts and uncertainties multiplied. He didn't understand what was going on. Not half of it. But he had to make a decision. Will grabbed the key from the ashtray and approached the woman.

"What's your name?"

"Jojo." She shifted her right leg off the bed.

"Jojo who?"

"Joanne Joleena. *Jojo.* Get it?"

"Hey, look — I don't need the attitude." He examined the key and the handcuff fastened to the bedpost. It took a moment to determine how they fit together.

"All right. Just unlock me," she pleaded with another gasp of exasperation. "Please."

Finch unlocked the cuff from the post and took it in his left hand.

"What are you doing?"

He noticed that she had two script tattoos on her forearms. One read *Forever Young.* The other, *Love Now.* "Where are your clothes?"

"In the bathroom."

He locked the free cuff around his right wrist and slipped the key into the half pocket in his jeans. "Okay, let's get you dressed."

"What the fu—"

"Come on." He yanked on the cuff and pulled her toward the bathroom. "Let's get going before it's too late."

CHAPTER TWO

"TAKE MY HAND." Finch grasped Jojo's left hand in his right and draped his jacket over the handcuffs that bound them together. "Anyone asks, and we're on a date. Okay?"

He stepped into the elevator car and pressed the "L" button.

"I said, *okay?*"

"Yeah. Whatever."

Jojo stood a foot shorter and weighed about a hundred pounds less than Finch. She wouldn't be able to resist whatever decisions he made. In the lobby he found a back door that led into an alley. From there he steered them along Washington Street and away from the emergency crews still managing the crowd on the corner sidewalk. Five minutes later, they sat side by side at a table in the San Sun Restaurant in Chinatown.

The waitress brought them a pot of tea and two shallow cups.

"You want to eat?" he asked.

"Yeah, I'm famished."

He passed her the menu and told her to choose something. This was the first opportunity he had to study her, and he soon realized that Jojo could be in real trouble. Her punk hair and pale face weren't a Hollywood fantasy job. She appeared to be twenty-five, but he guessed she was in her late teens. When she glanced up from the menu, he could see a small part of her right front incisor tooth had broken away at the tip. When she saw him stare, she flicked her tongue across her teeth and turned her chin toward him with an expression of defiance.

"What?" she asked.

"Nothing."

"Okay, so I broke my tooth last week." She seemed to think about it as if she needed to dredge up an explanation. "I fell and hit the sidewalk, all right?"

Finch considered the probabilities. A week ago Jojo cracked her tooth against the pavement. Tonight a man flies out a window and hits the concrete next to the curb. Two sidewalk impacts within a week. She didn't seem to detect the coincidence. "Sure. Fine. What do you want to eat?"

"Chicken fried rice." She pushed the menu aside with her free arm and braced her chin in the palm of her hand.

Finch waved for the waitress and ordered the fried rice and a bowl of wonton soup for himself.

"All right, Jojo." He tipped his head back toward that apartment building. "What was that about?"

"A queen-sized royal fuck-up."

"Yeah? That's already pretty clear. Where's See-See?"

A hint of surprise crossed her face. "You know him?"

Finch didn't remind her that she'd called out for someone named See-See after he entered the apartment.

"Through business," he said. A guess.

"Yeah. Sure," she said with a smirk. "You like pushing girls on strangers? I don't think so." This insight seemed to inspire a question of her own. "Look, who *are* you? And what were you doing up there?"

He paused to consider where this might be headed. What he should tell her, what to hold back.

"Will Finch."

"Finch?" A laugh slipped from her mouth. "Like the bird?"

He grimaced. The old high school taunting, still alive and well. "How 'bout we get back to you. Why were you stripped and cuffed to the bed?"

She shook her head in a gesture of humiliation. A long band of her hair fell across her face. It took a few seconds before she could gaze at him again. "I got a better question, Finch. Why am I still cuffed to you?"

He leaned forward and narrowed his eyes. "Because I've got the key, Jojo. Because I'm the one who saved you, remember? And because at any minute, I can get the cops over here and report that you're an accessory to murder." He continued to stare at her and then added, "Got it?"

"Murder?" Her tongue stuck in her throat.

"Yeah. That's what it's called when See-See pushed that guy out the window onto the street. Which brings me to the next question. Who the hell is the dead guy?"

"...Murder..." Jojo was unable to dismiss the gravity of what had happened, especially now that she realized, in the eyes of the law at least, she was implicated. "Look, I got no idea. I saw him like, *once*. He stuck his fat face through the door to make sure I was cuffed. Like just the way he wanted. Then he went back into the living room with See-See."

"Wait a sec." Will held up his free hand. "What's that mean? See-See?"

"All the girls call him See-See." She waved a hand. "Because he told us he could always see what we were up to. And it was like, basically true."

"All right, go on."

"Then I heard some sort of scuffling, then a scream and then … nothing. See-See never came back to get me. I heard him leave in a big hurry and that was it. *Gone.*"

A big hurry, Finch thought. So big that See-See didn't bother locking the apartment door.

"Then I started clicking that light. That's the full story." She shrugged with a hint of disbelief and a loop of hair fall across her face again. "Then you showed up."

The waitress delivered the fried rice and wonton soup with a set of chopsticks and a soup spoon. Jojo studied her plate with a sneer of disgust. She stared at the waitress. "I need a fork," she whined and held up her cuffed hand — still hidden under the jacket — to illustrate that she was disabled. "A fork. Not *fucking chopsticks.*" She threw the chopsticks against the floor, and they skittered to the far wall.

"Sorry." Finch shrugged at the waitress to suggest he was an older brother indulging an impudent child. "Sorry," he repeated. "She's had a bad night."

The waitress picked up the chopsticks and returned with a fork. They both began to eat. Jojo consumed her meal with ravenous hunger and apart from the sound of her moans of satisfaction, they ate in silence.

When he finished his soup, Finch set the bowl aside and

wiped his lips on a paper napkin. "All right. Tell me who the dead guy is."

Jojo forked a piece of chicken into her mouth. As she chewed, she shook her head. "I told you. I don't know. Some guy named Gio that See-See was supposed to hook me up with. We'd done it two or three times before with other johns. He makes videos of us doing it. Then he charges them for the tapes."

"How much?"

"Dunno." She shrugged. "But none of that happened tonight. Believe me, the guy never touched me."

Finch considered this. A blackmail set-up that somehow escalated into a hit job. Somebody had made a mistake. Probably See-See realized it when his victim flew out the window. In a panic, he fled the apartment without Jojo. And without locking the door.

"What's See-See's last name?"

"I don't know."

"Where does he live?"

"Don't know that either."

"Yeah?" He tipped his head to one side. "I don't believe you."

"Well, Finch, then why don't you fucking fly away home. You think I care?" She slipped another forkful of rice into her mouth.

"Where do you live?"

She ignored the question, and her defiance returned. Will doubted he could draw any more information from her and she finished the last of her meal in silence. Let her enjoy it, he thought. Soon things will be much more difficult for her.

"So, Jojo," he said when she nudged her dinner plate to the edge of the table. "You have a choice to make. You can choose door one" — he held up his left hand and swiveled it palm out, then back — "or door two."

"Fine. Door two. Just take off the cuffs and I'll get out of your life."

He smiled and continued with his analogy. "One, you can either take me to where See-See lives right now" — he swung his hand in the air again — "or go through door two, and we pay a visit to the local cop shop."

Her eyes widened with disbelief. "Well, door one is locked shut. And if you think I can't play the police game as good as you — think again, mister."

Before he could reply, Jojo began screaming. She stood up and threw Finch's jacket to the floor and shot their cuffed hands in the air.

"Call the cops!" she screamed. *"He's kidnapping me! Call the cops!"*

The restaurant manager approached the table and gazed at the scene unfolding before him. A frantic woman handcuffed to a man who bore an expression of meditative calm. The manager froze at the apparent contradiction.

Finch nodded at him. He pulled a twenty dollar bill from his pocket and set it on the table. He made an effort to soothe Jojo but when her frenzy broke into relentless crying, he knew she'd won.

"Okay, do as she says. Call the police," he conceded and then turned to the girl. In a flat, even voice he said, "Sit and relax, Jojo. They'll be here in a couple of minutes. Then you'll get your day in court."

CHAPTER THREE

THE SAN FRANCISCO Police Department's Central Station occupied the bottom floor and basement of a five-story parkade on Vallejo Street. Built in 1969, the facility was the oldest of ten SFPD stations spread throughout the city. The building exterior was composed of scores of vertical concrete bars that ran from the bottom floor to the top of the garage. Despite the best intentions to make Central a community resource, from the sidewalk it seemed more like a bomb-proof prison than a hub of civic pride.

Although Will Finch had never been in a police interview room before, Room 3 held only a few surprises. Years of watching TV cop shows as a teenager led him to believe the space would contain something more than a door, a mirrored glass window, a table and two chairs. But in Room 3 there were no intercom buttons, no electronic locks, no digital recorders. Apart from the video camera retrofitted to the ceiling with a vice clamp, the room appeared to be state-of-the-art for 1969.

While he waited for his interrogation, Will paced the dimensions in a toe-to-toe march along the length and width of the tiny box. Ten by fourteen feet. Even if you suffered from the mildest form of claustrophobia, you'd likely plead guilty to any number of crimes to secure your release from the room. In his case, Finch imagined that Jojo was cooking up a charge of kidnapping. Who knows, he asked himself, she might even be trying to pin the murder on him.

Another hour passed before Detective Richard Staimer entered the room and introduced himself. He was tall and lean, and his face held a taut, leathery grimace. A faded bruise and a few stitch marks sat below his right cheekbone. If he were a ranch hand, everyone would call him Slim or Hank. He settled himself in the metal chair next to the door and placed a manila file folder on the table.

"Okay, Mr. Finch, time for your side of the story. I'm interviewing you as a witness. If that changes, I'll be reading you your rights." He raised his eyebrows to indicate that Finch's situation was fluid, if not a potential sink-hole. "Do you understand?"

"Yes." He realized this could go either way. What he said now — and *how* he said it — would determine if he would walk away a free man.

"Good. So, what happened out there?"

Will exhaled a long breath. "Well, the last thing Jojo said to me was that I'd kidnapped her. I imagine that's what she told you, too. Maybe more. But it's not true."

He studied Staimer's face to see if this suggestion had an impact. He blinked and rolled his hand to urge Finch to continue.

"The fact is, I rescued her. About ten minutes after a group of teenagers found the body of someone who'd fallen to the sidewalk on Washington Street. Then I noticed a light flashing next to an open window on the eleventh floor above the Bank of America. I went up to the room. It was unlocked. I heard a cry and entered the apartment. That's when I found her partially naked and handcuffed to a bed."

"Whoa." He held up a hand. "You said some kids found the corpse? And *then* you went up?"

"That's right. I was there when he landed. Just behind them."

"You know these kids?"

"One of them. Alice Winkler."

"Do you know how to reach her?"

"Give me a slip of paper and a pen, and I'll give you her number."

Detective Staimer pursed his lips with a determination that suggested he was prepared to follow the new lead. He pulled a pen and palm-sized notepad from his jacket pocket and passed them to Will.

He wrote the information on the first page and felt a glimmer of hope, grateful now that he'd taken two seconds to commit Alice's number to memory.

Staimer checked his watch. "All right, give me some more time, and I'll get back to you on this." He stood and put his hand on the doorknob then turned back to Will. "Want some water?"

"I'd prefer a coffee."

Staimer coughed up a laugh. "Uh, not from here, you don't."

Finch smiled at that. "Okay, I'll settle for the water."

Staimer nodded and left the room.

Over the next hour, Finch slumped his torso over the table-top and rested his head on his forearms. He managed to doze in a sort of half-sleep but never fell into unconsciousness.

"All right," Staimer said as he returned to the interview room. He passed Finch a bottle of Evian water. "The Winkler kid backed you. So did two of her friends. No question, that helps you. But tell me about the handcuffs. And why the hell did you cuff yourself to the girl and then take her to the San Sun Restaurant?"

Will realized that he was now in control of a credible narrative. He uncapped the water bottle and took a deep drink. Then step-by-step he took Staimer through the entire story. From cuffing the girl to himself in the apartment, riding down the elevator, slipping out a back exit and along the block to the San Sun Restaurant. His goal, he told Staimer, was to take Jojo to safety and away from the threat posed by whoever threw the victim out the open window. "Once I determined that Jojo was safe," he concluded, "I intended to bring her with me to the first cop I could find. Believe me, I had no interest in being charged with accessory to murder."

"And she knew that?"

"I told her that's what I was going to do." He decided to omit the first option he'd offered her: To choose door number one and lead him to See-See's apartment.

"But then she beat you to the punch."

"Yeah, that was the only play she made. Jumping up and screaming that I'd kidnapped her." He shrugged. "To be honest, I didn't see it coming. You should talk to the restaurant manager and waitress. I think they saw my side of events. I didn't force her to do anything. Hell, I bought her a plate of chicken fried rice."

"Yeah, I already talked to them." Staimer folded his arms across his chest to suggest they were about to change course. "So who are you, Finch?"

"What?"

He opened his file folder. "It says here you spent four years in the US Army. Half the time in Abu Ghraib." He shifted his gaze from the file. "Awarded the Distinguished Service Cross. That right?"

Finch nodded. While he'd been made to wait, apparently someone in the SFPD had pulled together his bio. He wondered what they had on him. And what they'd missed.

"Then discharged two years ago." He closed the file folder. "I mean, what's your story? How do you go from that" — he tipped a hand to the file — "to cuffing yourself to an underage prostitute in an apartment in Chinatown rented to someone named Ray Smith?"

Ray Smith. Finch wondered if the name was genuine or bogus.

"Yeah, sounds like a back-flip, I know." Finch laughed as though he couldn't quite believe it himself. "Look, after Iraq I needed a change of direction. The fact is, I'm not so different than a lot of guys who finish a tour in the sandbox. Some of us started to question things."

Staimer nodded with a glower that said, go on.

"So I decided to go to grad school. I'd done journalism in college. When Berkeley offered me a spot in their MJ program,

I jumped at it. By the end of December, I'll be done. And looking for a job."

"As a reporter. Working on stories like this." He opened his hand to indicate the story was still unfolding. "That's why you took the girl with you. You wanted to squeeze out all the juice you could, right?"

Finch took a moment to consider this. Despite his cowboy appearance, Staimer was smarter than Finch had assumed.

"Maybe. Maybe not. My first instinct was to get both of us out of there — she said both of us could be killed. Besides, if I just released her, it presented one more risk that I could be charged as an accessory. And I didn't want her to run before you could talk to her. After the years I spent in Abu Ghraib, I learned the value of a thorough interview."

"You mean interrogation?"

Finch didn't know how to interpret this. At first, Staimer seemed to credit him for his service. Now came this slight shift. If he needed to, he could say that he'd never conducted any illegal interviews. In fact, he'd been assigned to Abu Ghraib Prison as an undercover military intelligence officer to determine what had gone so wrong at the prison. His cover was to serve as the regional Public Affairs Specialist. Otherwise known as a "Flak" to the international media who reported the stories of torture and forced confessions. But Finch could never disclose any of that. He'd been sworn to secrecy and more important, promised himself to bury the past.

"I prefer the word 'interview.' Obviously, others dispute that. In any case, tell me how I stand here, Detective Staimer. Am I under arrest?"

D. F. Bailey

Staimer shrugged and pursed his lips again, a mixed gesture that Finch couldn't decipher. He decided that Staimer would make a good poker player. Impossible to read his hand. Or his loyalties.

"No, not today." He held up a finger. "But I've got to warn you, Mr. Finch, if the girl goes to trial, you'll be called to testify. Then all bets are off. In the meantime, if you hear anything more on this, call me."

He passed Finch his business card. As he tucked the card into his shirt pocket, Will felt a wave of relief flood through his chest and arms.

"Thanks, Detective." He placed his hands flat on the table and pushed himself out of the chair. "By the way, did you get the name of the guy who went out the window?"

Staimer snorted with a glare of disbelief and stood up. "I can't believe you're asking me that."

"No?"

"Why don't you read about it in the morning papers?"

"All right." Finch absorbed the sarcasm and knew not to press him.

Staimer picked up the file folder and opened the door for Finch.

"And do me a favor. Don't let me see you back here again."

"Like you said, 'not today.'" Finch tried to suppress a smile. "Or at least not until you upgrade the coffee."

CHAPTER FOUR

THE HEAVY RAIN that forecasters had predicted over the last two days now began in earnest. Finch pulled his hoodie over his head, zipped up his leather jacket, and made his way to the Montgomery Street BART station. From there he took the subway under the Bay and over to Berkeley.

By the time he entered the apartment he shared with his fiancée, she'd already left for work. After he'd arrived at the SFPD station for questioning, he'd been allowed to make a call and left a message on their landline answering machine. Now he found a note from her on the kitchen table.

Are you alright? If you don't call me by noon, I'll get John Biscombe on this. Call me ASAP! xo xo xo

John Biscombe had just graduated from Berkeley Law and was starting to build his practice. Everyone knew that growing a private law firm from scratch was risky, but he'd managed to land a client during his first week out. Perhaps Finch would be next on his roster. Hopefully not, he told himself.

He called the Doe Memorial Library and managed to reach

Cecily on the second ring.

"Are you okay?" Her voice held a note of desperation — and relief. He immediately regretted putting her through the stress of his absence. Their first night apart during six months of living together hadn't unfolded as he'd imagined.

"I'm fine. It's nothing." He walked to the sliding glass doors that led to the balcony and gazed across the parking lot onto Dwight Way. "Like I said on the message, I was witness to something, so the police had to question me."

"Something? *What* something?"

Finch heard the doubtful tone. She had a good ear for things left unsaid.

"It was crazy." He glanced away as the memory of the death on the street washed over him. "I was on the way home after meeting with Bisk, Jerry and Phil at Cafe Zoetrope, when this guy landed on the sidewalk in front of me."

"What?"

"Yeah. Horrible. From eleven floors up. Four kids were right there, too. They shouldn't have seen it — but what can you do? There it was."

"Oh my God. Are you all right?"

"Yeah. But the police wanted to question me, and it took way longer than I imagined." He paused to think how much more he should reveal on the phone and decided to leave it at that for now. "Look, I'm going to get some sleep and then finish the last edit of my thesis."

"Okay." She sighed. "See you for dinner?"

"Sure. Eight o'clock at Kiraku?"

"Mmm, yes," she purred. She loved sushi and ate it at least

once a week.

He laughed. "Then I'll bring you back here for dessert."

"Ha-ha. *Dessert*, huh?" She chuckled at that. "Well then, you better be good to me. No more nights out."

"For sure. I guarantee it."

※

After he ended the call with Cecily, Will showered, shaved, brushed his teeth and made his way to the bedroom. He glanced at the clock and decided to take a short nap. Finch set the alarm for noon and slipped under the covers. Moments later he fell into a heavy, dreamless sleep.

The sound of the rain hitting the roof woke him at twelve-thirty. He checked the alarm and silently cursed himself when he discovered that he'd set it for midnight by mistake. A symptom of sleep deprivation, he thought and forced himself out of bed. By one o'clock he was sitting in the Caffe Mediterraneum — the funky, purposefully misspelled cafe on Telegraph Avenue — sipping an Americano and leafing through the *San Fransisco Post*. On page seven he found a three-paragraph story about the death on Washington Street.

FALL FROM 11ᵗʰ FLOOR PROVES FATAL

Local real estate investor, Gio Esposito, fell from the eleventh floor of an apartment tower on the corner of Washington and Stockton Streets last night.

Adrian Shouldice, an associate of Esposito, stated that his colleague had become dispirited following a series of recent business failures. "Last time I saw him, he was flat-out de-

pressed. His last two business deals failed due to the collapsing mortgage market," said Shouldice who shared a co-op office with Esposito on Sacramento Street.

An online report from the San Francisco Police Department states that they searched the apartment from which Esposito fell but could find no suicide note. They are interviewing a woman who may have witnessed the incident, but police did not reveal her identity.

Finch read the story a second time. He now had a few new facts in hand: the name of the victim, his occupation, and the name of his associate. Furthermore, Detective Staimer had revealed that the apartment was rented to someone named Ray Smith. Likely a pseudonym, but worth checking.

As he read the story a third time, he realized the *Post* had uncovered a few details, but none of the background facts. Nothing about Jojo handcuffed half-naked to the bed. No mention of See-See. And no reference to the unlocked apartment door. He checked his watch: 1:25. He guessed he could make it back to San Fransisco and over to the *Post* editorial office in a little less than an hour.

He stuffed the newspaper into his courier bag, pulled the hoodie over his head and made his way through the rain to the Downtown Berkeley BART station.

※

Wally Gimbel was a big man. Big face, big shoulders, big voice. But more striking than any other feature was his smile. It broke open on his face, wide and ear-to-ear — a smile full of joy and the love of life. The laugh that came with it was big, too. But then he quickly cut off the laugh while the smile lingered. As if the audio portion of a marvelous video clip had been stopped short. The effect took Finch by surprise. As suddenly as he felt embraced by Wally, he wondered if he'd just been shown the door.

Wally had told Finch a rambling story about Bernice Walden. About the 1987 staff Christmas party when she'd gone to the bathroom at Johnny Foley's Irish House and emerged with her pantyhose hiked over the back of her skirt. Before Bernice could walk to the bar and order another Guinness, Wally alerted her to her "clothing malfunction." But not before he cackled with his bearcat laugh. She'd grabbed him by the earlobe and made him pledge never to tell a soul. It was a promise he didn't keep. In fact, Finch suspected that Wally Gimbel broke this promise quite regularly.

"So how is Bernice treating you?" Wally asked.

Twenty years after the staff party escapade, Bernice Walden was now Finch's thesis advisor at UC Berkeley Graduate School of Journalism. Decades earlier she'd worked as a beat reporter stationed beside Wally Gimbel at *The San Fransisco Chronicle.* A year later, he snapped up the offer to serve as the arts editor at the *Post.* And soon after Wally's departure, she moved on to teach at Berkeley.

"Bernice treats me well enough," Finch said. He was pleased that her name had served as a passport to get him into Wally's office.

"So our front desk said you know something about last night's suicide." He tipped his hand toward Dixie Lindstrom, the receptionist stationed outside his door. "She said you were there. What've you got?"

Now that the conversation had turned to business, Finch could see the practical side to Wally Gimbel. He'd spent the last five minutes telling his story about Bernice Walden, but now he didn't waste an extra second.

"I was there. After he hit the street, I went up to the apartment from where he was pushed." Will paused. He knew he had to pitch this in five sentences or he'd be out the door. "Mr. Gimbel, this was a murder. Gio Esposito was thrown through the window by someone named See-See. Why? Because it was a blackmail setup that went south."

Wally leaned back in his chair. He narrowed his eyes with an expression that told Finch he was skeptical. "And you know this how?"

"There was a woman in the apartment bedroom named Joanne Joleena. She was handcuffed half-naked to the bed. I released her and then interviewed her in a restaurant just down the block from the apartment."

Wally held out a hand as if he was bringing a line of traffic to a halt. "Hold it. This was a murder scene — and you released a witness? *So you could interview her?* You know you could be charged with obstruction. Maybe even accessory to murder."

He shrugged off the suggestion. "I was just cleared by the SFPD. I spent the night in one of their down-market interview rooms." He smiled, uncertain if Gimbel would appreciate the small joke. "As far as I know, they're still talking to Joleena. I think she's the woman named in your report." He pointed to the current edition of the *Post* on Wally's desk. "Here's the thing.

28

She knows who See-See is. I need to interview her and find him before they both disappear."

"All right." Wally tented his fingers together. "If what you're telling me is true, then I want to pull Olivia in here to interview you."

"Who's Olivia?"

"Olivia Simmons. The reporter who wrote today's story."

Finch hesitated. He hadn't anticipated this. "Mr. Gimbel, I —"

"Please, no formalities. Just call me Wally."

"All right ... Wally." He glanced away to compose himself. "Listen, I honestly think this is something that only *I* can do. I spent over an hour with this girl. I rescued her from God-knows-what when I led her out of that building. I've got a relationship with her. Look, I can break this story wide open."

"Maybe. But Olivia can handle all of that."

"Wally," he said leaning forward. *"I* want to write this story."

Wally blinked. "Sorry. We have staff writers to do that."

"Then I'll freelance it to you." His shoulders stiffened. "It's *my* story," he said as if this were the only justification he needed to claim it as his alone.

Wally lifted his hands, palms up, a gesture to say that was not an option.

"All right." Finch stood up. "Somehow I thought this might work. Sorry I wasted your time." He opened the office door. "I guess I'll take it over to the *Chronicle.*"

As he walked past the receptionist's desk, he heard Wally call out to him in his heavy voice. "Will."

He turned back to the editor.

"I want you to meet Dixie Lindstrom, the *Post* receptionist." He waved a hand and waited until Finch joined him. "Dixie, this is Will Finch."

They shook hands.

"Will's going to work on the story Olivia punched up this morning," Wally continued. "Draw up a standard freelance contract for him. After I sign it, give him a copy. Then introduce him to Olivia and give him a desk." He glanced back at Finch. "Do you need a desk?"

Surprised by the sudden shift in events, Finch tried to imagine what he needed. After a brief hesitation, he said, "I just need a phone."

"You don't have a phone?" Wally seemed genuinely bewildered, as if everyone under thirty should have a phone.

Finch gave him a look that said, so what do you care?

"All right. Give him a desk with a phone. The closer to Olivia the better." He swung from Dixie back to Finch. "And I want you to report to me on this story at least once a day until it wraps up. Got it?"

"Yes, Mr. Gimbel."

"And call me Wally." He shook his head to suggest that Finch was a slow learner, but maybe he could be tolerated if he produced. He returned to his office and closed the door.

Finch stared at Dixie for a moment, not quite sure what to say. He lifted both hands in the air as if he was trying to grasp something. "That was just weird."

"What was?"

"I offered to freelance the story for him. He refused. Then

… well, what you just saw."

"Welcome aboard." Her expression indicated that what might pass for weird in the outside world was standard fare inside the *Post*. "He was probably testing you. To see how much you wanted the job," she said as she dug through a file cabinet to fish out a freelance contract form. "That's all that counts here. The story."

She passed him the contract and a pen. He scanned it briefly, all three paragraphs, and signed it.

"Okay," she said. "Let's get you a desk with a phone."

CHAPTER FIVE

FINCH DIDN'T HAVE a cellphone, but he did have a laptop. After he settled at the desk next to Olivia Simmons, he pulled his Dell computer from his courier bag and brought up the contact page for the SFPD Central Station on his screen. He picked up the landline telephone handset and called the non-emergency number. The receptionist passed his call to the desk sergeant who advised him that Joanne Joleena was still in custody.

"Has she been charged?" he asked.

"I can't disclose that."

"Can we bail her out?"

"Not until she's charged."

A catch-22. Finch tried to resolve the puzzle. "So she's still in custody but hasn't been charged. Have I got that right?"

"Correct." The desk sergeant's voice revealed that he'd run out of patience. "Sir, I've got to move on."

Finch sighed and hung up. He needed Jojo to identify See-See and where he lived. Will needed to talk to her, if not on the phone, then as a visitor in the SFPD holding tank. He imagined that she'd soon be charged as an accessory. But to what? Murder, blackmail, prostitution?

32

As of now Jojo and See-See were effectively off his radar. And unless he could contact them, his freelance gig would evaporate. As far as he was concerned, in less than a day the story had gone from red-hot to stone-cold. He glanced around the editorial room to settle his mind.

About thirty desks filled the windowless space, but roughly a third of them appeared to be unoccupied. Likely the result of a shrinking subscriber base that had shuttered hundreds of newsrooms across the country in the past decade. The *San Francisco Post* was just one more victim of the digital revolution.

However, the other twenty desks hummed with the quiet activity of reporters typing on their keyboards, conducting interviews on their phones, or chatting in groups of two or three. Beside him, Olivia Simmons hung up her phone and turned her attention to her computer terminal. Finch caught her eye.

"Olivia Simmons, right?"

"You got it." She stood up and stretched her back. She wore a navy blue pantsuit, a tan blouse and matching tan shoes with flat heels. "You new here?"

"Just in for a day or two. I'm Will Finch." They shook hands, and Will considered how to continue. "Wally wants me to follow up on that guy who went through the window last night. Gio Esposito?"

"Wally assigned you to this?" Simmons's eyes narrowed. "Really?"

Finch detected a wariness. "Listen, you interviewed Adrian Shouldice. He shared Gio Esposito's office on Sacramento

Street, right?"

"Yeah ... so?"

Finch shrugged as if he needed a favor. "I need their office address."

"The address?"

"Right. For Gio Esposito's office."

"You're kidding me." Her expression took on an air of disbelief, and she sat down again.

"No. Dead serious. Ask Wally."

"Hang on." She tapped her fingers on the desk as if she had to consider the request. Then she picked up her phone and punched two numbers on the keypad with her index finger. She covered the mouthpiece with her hand and mumbled something in an intense whisper. After a brief conversation, she replaced the phone handset in the cradle, wrote something on a notepad, tore the sheet of paper from the pad and passed it to Finch.

"All right. Wally says you're legit."

Finch glanced at the paper and memorized Gio Esposito's office address. Then he turned back to her. "Thanks, Olivia. I owe you one."

She winced as though she'd just surrendered a valuable asset to a complete stranger. A rough-cut diamond she was about to shape and polish into a prized work of art. Gone.

"That's all I've got, Finch. Just don't come back asking for more. I have nothing else on this story."

※

An hour later, Will climbed the stairs in a renovated three-story walk-up built during the Depression era in the 1800 block on Sacramento Street. From the lobby directory, he determined

that most of the tenants were solo proprietors and serial entre-
preneurs struggling to make it to second base. A few real estate
agents, lawyers, and accountants occupied the first floor.
Above them, the professional sheen seemed to fade. The third
floor housed a mixed bag of ad agencies, web site designers,
private investigators, forensic accountants — and at the far end
of the hall — Versatile Properties Group.

As he approached the VPG office, the door swung open. A
thick-set man, a little over six feet, stared at Finch. A surprised
glower crossed his face as if he were expecting to see someone
more familiar.

"Adrian Shouldice?" Finch put on a smile.

"Never heard of him," he said and brushed past Finch
without another word.

Finch caught the door before it closed, and stepped into the
reception area. Before him sat a middle-aged woman at a desk.
She had gray hair streaked with bands of pink and blue. Pressing a phone to her ear, she acknowledged Finch with a wave of
her hand. The plastic nameplate on her desk read "Shirley." He
stood before her and studied the surroundings while she finished her call.

The reception area was tidy, but like the rest of the
building, aching for a do-over. Above Shirley's shoulder, a
wood panel listed the six tenants of the shared office space.
Each had a name engraved on a two-by-six-inch brass plaque.
Esposito & Associates was third from the top. The bottom plate
read: Adrian Shouldice, Mortgage Broker.

Shirley hung up the phone and offered him an inviting
smile. "Can I help you?"

"You can. I heard Adrian is in. Can I go back?" Finch smiled and pointed to the inner hallway.

"Can I tell him who's visiting?"

"Oh, sorry." Will's voice rose in an apologetic tone. "Sure. Tell him it's Will Finch."

"He knows you?"

"I hope so." He grinned again, pleased that he didn't have to tell an outright lie.

She picked up the handset to her phone, pressed an intercom line and mentioned Finch's name. She put the phone back in its cradle and tipped her head to the back offices. "He doesn't remember you but said his three o'clock canceled. So, he can see you now."

"Great. Lucky for me." As he made his way along the narrow corridor, he paused at the office marked Esposito & Associates. He tried the doorknob, realized it was unlocked — but then continued down the hall to the third office. When he reached Adrian Shouldice's door, he tapped lightly on the wood frame.

"Come in."

Finch stepped into the room and closed the door behind him.

"Mr. Shouldice?

"Yes?"

"I'm Will Finch." He shook Shouldice's hand. "From the *Post*. I'm doing a follow-up on Gio Esposito's death."

"Really? I just spoke to —"

"Olivia Simmons. I know." Finch cut him off to block any objections. He laughed to suggest they were both victims of a newspaper SNAFU. Standard fare. "I'm digging for a little more background on Esposito. By the way, sorry to hear that Olivia had to break the news of his death to you."

"Well. What can you do?" He shrugged off the apology. "It's not like I knew him very well."

"No?" Finch studied him a moment. He wore a chestnut brown tweed vest, beige shirt, and a burgundy-colored tie. Not the trendiest style, but it conveyed the appearance of a conservative businessman who managed the kind of trickle-down investments that generated money while he slept.

"No. I never met any of his friends or family. I think he was from Missouri." Shouldice rolled his head from side to side. "Frankly, the guy was a bit of a mystery man to me."

Finch held up his hand to suggest a change in direction. "Look, sorry to come in here on short notice, but I just picked up this story. Adrian, do you mind if I sit down and make a few notes?"

"Sure. Your timing couldn't be better. My three o'clock just canceled."

"So I heard." He tipped his head toward the reception area, a signal that he'd caught the news from Shirley. "How long did you know him?"

"Seven, maybe eight months?" Shouldice glanced at the ceiling as if the answer might be inscribed on the cracked plaster. As he raised his head, Finch could see Shouldice's double chin flatten into a single plane.

"No...nine months. Esposito moved into Bill Sovena's office after Bill retired in February."

Finch took a steno pad and pen from his courier bag. "So

how does this work? Is everyone here a partner in Versatile Properties Group?"

"No, we're all independent. VPG is Shirley's company. We all rent space from her. We share a boardroom and the kitchenette, and she handles the front office for everyone. She only rents to people in some facet of real estate. Realtors, insurance, mortgage brokers like me. Keeps the brand clear."

"I see. And Esposito was handling real estate investments for corporate clients, right?"

"It was more focused than that." He leaned forward a few inches and propped his elbows on the desk. "He was packaging deals."

"Packaging deals?"

"Yeah. MBSs. Mortgage-backed securities."

"And they are … what, exactly?"

He chuckled under his breath and checked his watch. "Got an hour?"

"Yeah, as a matter of fact, I do." Finch laughed as well. For the first time, he was breaking open new information on the story.

"You heard of Warren Buffet?'

Finch shrugged. "Who hasn't?"

"In 2003 Buffet called derivatives 'financial weapons of mass destruction.' These days, the financial WMDs are made up of bundles of Mortgage Backed Securities." Shouldice studied Finch's face to determine if he was following.

"Wait." Finch put his pen aside to consider this. "Didn't some bank in France refuse to bring any more of these things onto their books? Last summer, right?"

"Very good." Shouldice ran his tongue between his lips and nodded. "BNP Paribas. And in April, New Century Financial Corporation — America's second-largest subprime mortgage lender — went into bankruptcy. And in June, two Bears Sterns hedge funds ran into trouble. All because of real estate derivatives."

He now had Finch's complete attention. Over the next half hour, Shouldice described the situation as he saw it. The real estate market had peaked in 2006. Despite the slide in prices, the buying frenzy grew into a mindless orgy of speculation. Now the party was coming to a brutal end. However, the world's financial system had swallowed hundreds of billions in garbage mortgages that would soon default. When Shouldice saw that Finch had been duly impressed with the scale of the pending catastrophe, he summed up his story in four words: "There will be pain."

"And how did Gio Esposito fit into all of this?"

"Like I told you." He shook his head as if Esposito's fate had been sealed long ago. "He packaged special deals and sold them to investment syndicates. Hundreds of sub-prime, Mortgage Backed Securities. Everyone wanted them. *Demanded* them. They'd buy them and re-sell them in New York, London, Hong Kong for fifty percent markup. Esposito cooked them up like he was following a recipe. Two or three a month. When the pudding exploded," he said in mock surprise, "it made quite a mess. Ultimately, he had to declare bankruptcy. Or was about to."

"But not before last night when he landed on the street." Finch could see a motive now. Someone needed Esposito to make good on money that had gone bad.

"Landed face first, from what I heard." Adrian Shouldice smiled, then glanced at Finch as if he wanted confirmation that his colleague had come to the worst possible end.

"Maybe," Finch said, but he didn't want to reveal what he'd seen on the corner of Washington and Stockton Streets. It was terrible enough recalling the moment of Esposito's death. No need to turn it into a cause for celebration.

※

Shouldice's phone rang and after he picked up the handset, Finch made a silent gesture that he'd gathered all the information he needed and would find his way out. Shouldice smiled, waved a hand and Finch slipped into the hallway and closed the door.

From the reception area, he could hear Shirley laughing on her phone. Finch walked to the opposite end of the corridor to the kitchenette. Facing it, a series of glass panels marked off what Finch assumed was the boardroom. Both spaces were empty.

He turned and retraced his path until he reached the door to Esposito's office. He tried the handle again. Still unlocked. He drew a breath, stepped inside and eased the door closed. He turned on the ceiling light and examined the locking mechanism on the door lever. A built-in thumb bolt. He turned it clockwise and tested it. The door was now locked.

Unlike Shouldice's office, Esposito's workspace didn't have an exterior window. Instead, a three-by-five foot photo-poster was tacked to the wall opposite Esposito's desk. The photograph offered a sunlit view of a lake filled with century-old wooden boats. A caption read: "Lake of the Ozarks Boat Show, 2005." Finch imagined Esposito gazing at the poster from time to time, dreaming of his life back in Missouri. The Show Me State.

Will chuckled to himself and sat at the desk. "All right, Esposito, now show me what the hell happened to you."

He drew his Canon Powershot camera from his courier bag. The camera was a birthday present from Cecily, and for the first time, Finch was about to use the ultracompact for business purposes.

A green ink blotter with an opaque plastic cover lay across the arborite desktop. On the right corner of the blotter sat a green coffee mug inscribed with white letters that stated "Money I$ Everything." The mug held a quarter cup of cold, black coffee. A gray desk phone sat on the left corner. The phone wasn't quite state-of-the-art, but it had a display screen, and Finch scrolled through a list of recent calls. Ten numbers came up, and then the series began to repeat as he clicked the down arrow button. He tightened the focus on this camera lens and captured the set of ten numbers in two shots.

Next to the phone sat an old-school, circular Rolodex file that held hundreds of business cards stapled to the two-by-four-inch cards. When he considered this, Finch wondered if Esposito had a computer. If he'd been bundling sub-prime mortgages — two or three of them a month, according to Shouldice — Finch couldn't imagine Esposito functioning without a computer or laptop. He opened the three drawers on each side of the desk and found nothing but paper files, correspondence, bills, and papers about the Chapter 11 Bankruptcy filings for Esposito & Associates. He took pictures of the most recently dated legal documents, and several of the bills marked "Past Due."

On the wall opposite the door, a small futon sofa squatted under a framed certificate that identified Esposito as an accredited investment advisor by ICI Realtor Institute. Finch stood up and took a picture of the document. Next to the futon, he could see a power outlet and the ethernet cable for an internet connection. The cable lay on the carpet next to the desk. Again, he couldn't find a laptop or any peripherals. No laptop cover, no mouse, no printer.

It was possible that Shirley provided printing services in the reception area and Finch made a note to check for a printer on his way out. In the meantime, he decided to thumb through the Rolodex for any contacts that seemed irregular. He sat at the desk again and began his search. Most of the cards came from investment firms, banks, mortgage brokers (including one from Adrian Shouldice) real estate firms and lawyers. Nothing struck his curiosity, and after ten minutes, Finch set the Rolodex aside.

The bookcase provided the only other area of interest. It stood against the wall next to the door. Finch assumed it was an Ikea product, one of those unpronounceable brands that sold in the millions around the world. He nosed through the books, all of them industry guides, references and source documents. Between the second and fourth row of books stood a shelf reserved for knick-knacks and memorabilia. The most personal item was a framed picture of Esposito standing on a lakeside dock holding a fishing rod in his right hand. He stood tall, a big man who appeared to be over six feet according to the vertical measure painted onto a wharf piling that rose from the dock. From his left hand, he gripped a flathead catfish by the gills. The gauge showed that the fish was at least three feet long. Esposito's face bore a contented smile. At least the dead man had once enjoyed his lot in life.

Beside the photograph sat a collection of coffee mugs and some real estate convention swag. Orlando in 2003, San Diego in 2004, Portland in 2005, and San Francisco in 2006. Maybe after the 2006 convention, Esposito had decided to locate his business in The Bay Area.

After he completed his survey, Finch stood at the door and tried to piece together what he'd seen. The desk arrangements suggested that Esposito was right-handed: coffee mug on the right along with the Rolodex file and phone on the left. The room was orderly — but almost devoid of personality. Esposito had been a clean and tidy soul. Finch found it odd that the mug still held a splash of coffee without Esposito washing it up. He'd apparently taken his laptop, but left the coffee unfinished.

He decided that any meaningful information would come from Esposito's last ten calls or whatever he could discover in the bankruptcy files and unpaid bills. As he stood at the door, he heard Shirley's shoes clicking along the hallway toward him. The walls were thin, and he could hear her talking to another woman. He checked to ensure that the thumb bolt was locked. It was. Then he stood against the wall beside the book-case, the only hiding place at hand if the door swung open.

"I've been told we've got to go through probate, first," Shirley said in a firm voice. "Then I can rent Esposito's office. It could all take forever."

He heard a key struggling to fit into the lock.

"Damnit. Wrong key," Shirley said and retreated along the hall with her guest.

Finch took the opportunity to open the door and step into the corridor. He reset the thumb lock, closed the door behind him and tiptoed back toward Shouldice's office. When he turned, he saw Shirley and a uniformed female SFPD officer in her mid-forties approaching him.

"We'll see if this works," Shirley said to the cop and slipped the key into Esposito's office lock. "Yes. There we go."

He smiled and eased past the women on his way to the office reception area. Next to Shirley's desk stood a Xerox Phaser printer—a workhorse that could churn out print copies for a dozen offices. Satisfied that Esposito didn't need a printer, only one question remained unanswered. Where was the dead man's laptop?

As he made his way down the steps to Sacramento Street, he realized that he'd just missed a close call. The fact that the SFPD was searching Esposito's office demonstrated that they were still probing the circumstances surrounding his death. The case was still open. Likely Detective Staimer had uncovered something critical from Jojo.

Finch knew he had to talk to her and now a new idea came to him.

CHAPTER SIX

FINCH GAZED THROUGH the space of the Hawaii West Bar. A man dressed in a floral shirt restlessly tapped a plastic straw against the edge of his bottle of Miller Highlife. Another customer sat next to the front door muttering into an empty highball glass. Opposite him, the bartender stood alone reading a paperback as he leaned on the wood rail next to the till. Above the rack of liquor bottles, a muted TV monitor broadcast the most recent events concerning the financial troubles on Wall Street.

In the far corner, Finch waited for his lawyer friend, John Biscombe. Will had never heard of the Hawaii West before, but it was an agreeable place to sit out the rain. More important, it was just a few doors away from the SFPD Central Station on Vallejo Street. He'd called Biscombe from the bar phone and spent the past forty minutes nursing a Heineken beer and gnawing on some chicken wings. While he waited, he began to organize his thoughts on his laptop. He sensed that the Esposito story would change and evolve as he worked through the breaking events. Until he could see the direction ahead, he compiled a list of the facts, conjectures, and possibilities.

D. F. Bailey

• *The cops continue to question Jojo.*
• *The cops continue to investigate Gio Esposito.*
• *Esposito murdered in a bungled frame-up?*
• *The killer fled and left the door to the crime scene un-locked. Why?*
• *The killer's loyalty to Jojo is zero.*
• *Jojo knows more than she lets on. Her loyalty to the killer: 110%.*

He tried to envision the jigsaw puzzle before him. A vital puzzle piece concerned Esposito's unlocked office door. Also the open door to the apartment where he'd been thrown to his death. It had to be a coincidence, Finch told himself. But as he sat at the corner table sipping his beer and adding this detail to his list, he began to wonder about the odds. *Two* unlocked doors. Was it probable? He knew it was the sort of question no one could answer decisively. You either believed in coincidence, or you didn't. Things are either evolving in a state of random selection, or they're meant to happen. Darwinian or preordained.

Finch shook his head. He was inclined to the Darwinian view. But that only made things more incomprehensible. As he mulled over the options, John Biscombe entered the bar and peered through the dank gloom in Finch's direction. Will waved him over to his table.

Last fall Will met John Biscombe on a double date with Cecily's friend, MaryAnne. He was tall, fit and good-looking. In his undergraduate years, he'd been on the UCLA baseball

46

team and still had the deep tan to prove it. He smiled often and had the sort of charm that Finch usually considered with suspicion. Will imagined that he'd grown up surrounded by aquamarine swimming pools, ski lodge condos, and season tickets to the LA Dodgers. He was surprised to learn that Biscombe's parents divorced when he was ten, after his father had lost his job with AT&T. He'd made his way through college on a sports scholarship and working six-hour shifts at Starbucks. During the first two summers of his law degree, he'd worked on an uncle's fishing seiner out of Tillamook Bay in Oregon. Finch knew this was hard, dangerous work and he admired him for it.

"Bisk, glad you could make it." He stood up and shook the lawyer's hand. "Sorry, but we don't have time for another beer."

"No problem. You called me from the bar phone?" He crooked his thumb toward the payphone on the wall next to the dart board.

Finch grimaced and nodded. He knew what Biscombe was about to say. One more dig about his cellphone.

"Look at you." Biscombe put on a show of mock sympathy and wrapped an arm around Will's shoulder. "The league MVP catcher who bumbled an underhand toss. Just a rookie after all."

Biscombe flashed a smile. Then they both laughed, Biscombe with a little more zest than Finch as they pondered the story of how Will had lost his cellphone.

Two weeks earlier, on Saturday — Cecily's first day off from her new job — Will and Cecily had decided to take a mini-holiday. A day trip. The two of them boarded the ferry to cross San Francisco Bay from the Embarcadero to Sausalito. Twenty minutes into the voyage she clutched the crook of his elbow in her hand and pulled him close.

"Guess what?" she asked.

"What?" he said. The breeze tugged at her hair. Her face bore a worried demeanor that made him wonder.

"What?" he asked again.

"I'm pregnant."

The news took him by surprise — but he was elated. So delighted that he'd dropped to one knee and proposed to her on the spot. People began to notice. He looked up to her radiant face and popped the question. She nodded, and the crowd cheered. He passed his phone to a teenage boy and assumed he'd know what to do.

"Take a picture would you?" Will and Cecily stood next to the railing and wrapped their arms around one another. Kissed. And kissed again. More whoops from the crowd. The boy smiled as he held the phone out to Finch.

"I got a good one," he said. As Finch reached for the phone, he planted another kiss on Cecily's cheek. He felt the Nokia touch his fingers, then slip. As he turned away from Cecily, he fumbled badly. The phone bounced in his hand — once, twice — and flipped overboard. A collective moan went up from the crowd.

"That's terrible," said a bystander. She wore thin leather gloves and held a child by his hand. Perhaps her grandson. "I hope that's not bad luck."

"Yeah, me too," Finch said. He tried to dismiss the idea. Will believed in all forms of luck, good and bad. Like a roll of the dice, he considered them part of the Darwinian matrix. So for the rest of that day, he wondered — could it be a bad omen?

"So when'll you get a new phone?" Biscombe sounded a little more sympathetic now.

"I dunno. When I get paid?" Finch rolled his shoulders and glanced away. During their phone conversation, Will had revealed that he'd landed a freelance contract with the *Post*. A paycheck would soon follow.

Thinking about the lost phone put him in a funk. Biscombe seemed to appreciate his friend's mood and decided to shift the topic.

"Hey, you ready for the game on Sunday?"

Biscombe loved baseball, especially the beer league they'd joined in May. He could play shortstop, left field or third base. While he never made the leap into the semi-pro circuit, his years on the UCLA team made him pretty adept.

"Of course. I wouldn't miss it."

"Good. Once Jerry confirms the game time, I'll call you."

"Sounds good."

"We're in the semis, man!" He held up his hand for a high-five and Finch gave him the slap.

"Okay." Finch felt the need to turn the conversation back to business. "I take it you're not too busy today."

"Busy enough. You know. Trawling the police reports looking for new clients."

When he graduated from law school, Biscombe had told Will and Cecily that he'd struck on the idea of scanning the traffic accident reports to scare up some personal injury law-suits. So far, the newly-minted lawyer had landed only one client.

"Well, I might have a live one for you."

"Yeah?" Biscombe straightened the knot in his tie. "Big money?"

"More likely *no* money." Finch packed his laptop into his courier bag.

"Pro bono, huh?" The corners of his mouth turned down. "Another one."

"That's why everyone calls you Mahatma Bisk."

They laughed again and made their way out of Hawaii West and across Vallejo to the jail. As they walked, Finch explained Jojo's situation — and his plan to set up a private conversation with her. Apart from Biscombe gaining access to Jojo and managing all the legal niceties, when the right time came, Finch would signal Biscombe to step aside and allow him to speak to Jojo.

"So you're asking me to *trust* you?"

"Always," Finch replied. "Always and forever."

※

Jojo appeared before Finch and Biscombe with a spark of hope on her face. When she recognized Will, however, the veneer of optimism faded. She dipped her head to one side, and a hank of blonde hair fell across her forehead and covered her right eye. A fascinating way to duck out of sight, Finch thought. He recalled observing the same habit back in the San Sun Restaurant last night. Whenever he pressed her for an answer, she dipped her head and let the hair cover her eyes. A personal tic.

"So they let you out, huh," she mumbled.

Finch nodded. "Jojo, this is John Biscombe. He's a lawyer."

"Lawyer? Can you get me out of here?" Her mood brightened. "Get me bail or something?"

"Let's step over here," Biscombe said and led Finch to the edge of the twenty-foot span of steel bars that separated the prisoners from their visitors. Jojo followed along on her side of the barrier. Four other inmates stood at the edge of the cage and spoke to their lawyers, family members or friends. There were no chairs on either side of the bars. Each section of the partitioned room had a steel door. One for detainees to come and go. The other for people like Finch and Biscombe.

"From what the desk clerk told me, you haven't been charged with anything yet," Biscombe said. "So you don't need bail. Not so far, anyway."

She shook her head as though she sensed a conspiracy. "What the hell? Then how do I get out of here?"

Biscombe shrugged. "Habeas corpus. The law says if they don't charge you in forty-eight hours, they have to let you go."

"Yeah? And who holds them to that?"

"Me," Biscombe said.

"And if they do charge me with some faked-up sh—"

"Then I'll try to get you bail." Finch interrupted her, knowing it could be a stretch. Still, he knew he'd do what he could for her.

She brushed a hand over her face and pushed the hair bangs aside so that she could see him. "What's the catch, Finch?"

Will turned to his friend and gave him a wink.

"All right, this is where I need to disappear," Biscombe said and nodded to Finch. It was their prearranged signal. The moment when he could no longer be part of any bargaining between Finch and the girl. He walked to the door and turned his back to them.

Will leaned closer to the bars and whispered so that no one could hear them. "The catch is See-See."

"Jeezus. This again?" She glanced away but then appeared to give it a second thought.

"Ask yourself something, Jojo. Has See-See come down here to spring you?"

Her hair slipped over her eyes again.

"How about I answer that for you," Finch continued. "No, he hasn't. And why? Because he's blown town, Jojo. He's in too deep, and he knows it."

He saw a tear run down her cheek.

"I need to know two things, Jojo. See-See's last name and his address."

She drew a long breath. "You'll post bail for me?"

"If it comes to that, I'll try." He knew it was conditional, but he didn't want to lie to her. "And if you're charged and go to trial for something that rolls out of what happened in the apartment last night, I'll tell the truth about you if the judge calls on me."

"You will?" Her voice trembled with surprise as if no one had made an offer to help her before.

"Don't doubt it for a minute," Finch continued. "I'll be compelled to tell the truth. And I won't commit perjury — which is good news for you."

A moment of silence opened between them while she considered her situation. Finch didn't know which way she'd go.

"Jojo, I need See-See's last name and address." He hesitated and decided to press her one more time. "Give me those two things, and I'm here for you."

She released a long sigh. Finch thought she might have been holding her breath for the last minute while he laid out the deal for her.

"Look, I don't know it." Her face turned away. "Everyone just called him See-See."

"All right. Okay. It's not a problem." He glanced away while he adjusted his thinking. "Then what about his address?"

"I don't know. I know the street, but not the number. Down in the Mission on Cesar Chavez. At the end of Van Ness, where the two streets meet up. It's one of those old, nice-looking buildings with three floors. Green, with white trim. It's apartment seven." She hesitated and then added, "He keeps the key above the door."

Finch made a mental note of the location and apartment number and nodded to her. "You've made the right choice, Jojo."

"Have I?" She brushed her hair aside again and gazed into his eyes. He saw something new in her now, a sign of hope that would haunt him for a long time.

CHAPTER SEVEN

JOJO WAS RIGHT about See-See's apartment building. Ornate, colorful — but obviously worn and in need of some significant repairs. Finch figured it was once a tidy Victorian boarding house, one of the few that survived the 1906 earthquake. It had broad window frames that surrounded the bay windows that rose in four columns from the street up three stories to a flat rooftop. Unlike a lot of buildings in the Mission — now transformed by the money and energy of the Bay Area tech revolution — it hadn't been gentrified. At least not yet.

The building had two street-level entrances that stood about thirty feet apart. Both were gated and locked. Will climbed up the three steps to the north gate and examined the lock mechanism. It required a push button code which he knew he wouldn't be able to crack.

He decided to play a waiting game. He pulled the hoodie over his head to block the steady drizzle of rain and stepped over to the crosswalk lamppost. It was late afternoon, almost six o'clock, and he hoped someone would soon be coming or going from the building. He wasn't disappointed. Five minutes later a short, squat woman laden with three grocery bags passed him and crossed the sidewalk to the far entrance. Two children chattering in Spanish trailed behind her.

"Vamos, niños," she called to them.

Finch inserted himself between her and the boys.

"Can I help you with that?" he asked. When she glanced at him with a puzzled appearance, he said, "Puedo … ayudarte … con eso?" His Spanish was barely coherent, but she appeared to understand him and smiled.

"Si, señor."

He took her bags while she pressed the lock combination on the keypad. Then she herded the boys ahead of her, and they raced up the staircase.

"Gracias," she said and took her bags and began to climb upstairs.

Finch followed her then eased the gate back into its frame. The lock clicked shut. On the wall opposite the gated door, a building directory showed that apartment seven belonged to Seamus Henman. Finally, he had a full name. He eased along the first-floor hallway, a dark space heavy with stale, musty air. A single overhead light bulb barely illuminated the corridor. The quiet clatter of dishes, pots, and pans — the sounds of people preparing their evening meals — sounded through the old wooden doors that lined the hall. He reached the door that held a small rectangular metal plate with the number 7 embossed on its surface. Finch stood a moment and listened for any interior noise. He heard the faint sounds of rock music in the background.

He tried the door. Locked. Then he knocked lightly. No reply. He held his lips a few inches from the door and whispered, "See-See. I have a message from Jojo."

He waited for twenty, maybe thirty seconds. He pressed his ear to the door and heard the haunting rhythm of an electric organ. He now assumed that Seamus was either inside and would not respond to any visitors, or he'd left the apartment — or more wisely, left San Francisco.

Finch glanced at the top of the door and swept his fingers along the wood frame. A bronze key fell into his hand. Just as Jojo had predicted. He slipped it into the single cylinder lock and stepped into Seamus Henman's world.

"See-See?" The lights were off, the curtains pulled shut. "I need to speak with you."

Again, no reply. He closed the door.

He inhaled deeply and smelled the musty aroma of stale food. Now he could identify the music coming from a second room. The instrumental section in the middle of the Doors' melancholy dirge, *This Is The End.* He took a moment to gather his wits. He opened his courier bag, found his flashlight and latex gloves. He tugged the gloves over his hands and clicked on the light.

As he swept the light across the room, he surveyed a small, box-like apartment. To the right of the living room stood a kitchenette. To the left, an open door revealed a three-piece bathroom. Beside it, a second door led into what Will assumed was a bedroom. He moved into the kitchen area and quickly assessed the appliances. A two-burner stove top, a half-size refrigerator, a sink stacked high with dirty dishes. A pile of paper plates and discarded food scraps littered the countertop. Next to the sink sat a knife block that held only one knife and a sharpening rod. Beside the knife block the remains of a T-bone steak buzzed with five or six flies. He brushed his hand above the meat. The flies danced into the air and immediately returned to their feast.

He crossed the living room, a cramped space furnished with unmatched pieces. A stained sofa. A coffee table cluttered with discarded Fritos corn chip bags and empty Miller beer bottles. A faux-wood plastic stand holding a forty-inch flat screen Samsung TV. Whatever money Seamus Henman had saved — he'd invested it in the TV.

The background music shifted to Jefferson Airplane's *White Rabbit.* Finch stepped toward the source of the music, apparently a '60s FM rock station. The bedroom door was ajar, and Will nudged it open with the tip of his flashlight. Next to the bed stood a bedside table. On the table sat a mid-size Sony boombox blasting Grace Slick's rising voice: *"Feed your head, feed your head."*

Opposite the bed, a small man sat duct-taped to a straight-back wooden chair. The chair stood in the middle of a pool of blood. It took a moment for Finch to comprehend the horror confronting him. His first reaction — a gasp for air as his lunch rose from his stomach and burned toward his esophagus — propelled him to the bathroom. He gasped again and then choked back his spew. Then he recovered his composure and leaned against the sink and gazed at his face in the mirror.

"What the hell are you doing?" he asked himself. He shrugged off the question. He knew the answer. This was his chance. His turn. The corpse strapped to the chair in the bedroom was bad — but no worse than what he'd seen in Iraq. He focused his attention on his eyes staring back at him. After a few seconds, he was prepared to return to the bedroom and examine Seamus Henman's remains.

He leaned on the bedroom doorframe and studied the gagged and bound corpse. The body had bled out. The flesh on the neck and face had become an opaque veneer that revealed the narrow, blue tracks of the victim's lifeless veins.

"What a mess," he muttered as he braced a hand against the wall to steady himself. He knew he would have to find a telephone and call the police. Detective Staimer. But first, he had to ... what? An inner voice tried to suppress the effects of the adrenalin coursing through his veins. *Be rational. Document everything,* he told himself.

He pulled his Canon Powershot from his bag and returned to the living room. He switched the camera to the video function. Holding the flashlight in one hand and the camera in the other, he made a three-sixty sweep of the room. He followed the same procedure in the bathroom and bedroom where Seamus sat bound to the chair.

Then he reset the camera mode to single image. He drew a breath of courage and eased as close to the corpse as he could without stepping into the pool of blood. He held the camera about five feet from Seamus and adjusted the lens so that it provided a crisp view of the mutilated body.

As he photographed each wound, he described what he was witnessing, speaking aloud as if the words gave substance and reality to what otherwise seemed like a phantasmagorical nightmare. He knew that if he talked deliberately and accurately, he would remember the details when it came time to write the story for the *Post*.

"A serrated knife, a breadknife possibly, inserted below the right ribs, likely penetrating the liver."

He repositioned the camera and took another photograph. "A broad blade, possibly a meat cleaver, in the stomach."

He paused to draw a breath and then continued to shift, click the camera, and describe each laceration. "A carving knife in the victim's upper left ribs, probably penetrating the heart. A filleting knife drawn across the throat from left to right and set in place below the right jaw. A short paring knife buried in the left ear."

When he'd captured the final image, he sat for a moment on the unmade bed and gazed mindlessly at the upright cadaver before him. Finch could see that Seamus Henman, sitting bound in the chair, was not a big man. No taller than five-six. Maybe shorter. Someone had gagged his mouth and strapped him to the chair with duct tape. It wouldn't have taken much force to hold him down and then wrap the bands of tape around his wrists and ankles. Once that task was completed, the rest of job required only basic butchery skills.

"My God," he said as he imagined how the murder had played out.

Finch drew a hand over his face. He stared at the digital clock sitting on a three-legged stool next to the bed. 6:47. He'd planned to meet Cecily at Kiraku restaurant at eight. Not now. He knew she'd understand, but this was a sensitive time for her, and he didn't want to overwhelm her with his problems.

Careful not to disturb any evidence, especially the uneven ring of blood on the floor, he stood up and slipped back into the living room. A small table with collapsible wings stood next to the window. On one end of the table sat a landline telephone.

Under the phone base, he noticed a sheet of paper that had been creased and doubled over. He unfolded it. It was a fax transmission showing a gray-scale head-shot of a man staring directly into the camera lens. Finch studied the rectangular face. Beneath the narrow forehead, a pair of uneven eyebrows rode a heavy ridge, perhaps a bone deformity, that welled above his eyes. His lips were plumped as if he were about to spit on the floor. A Kirk Douglas dimple punctuated the middle of his chin. Something familiar about him puzzled Finch, but he couldn't resolve it.

At the bottom of the image, Finch could barely make out a ten-digit fax number. Apart from the numbers, there was no other text of any kind. He took a moment to focus his camera lens on the fax sheet and captured several images. With each shot, he made tiny adjustments to sharpen the definition of the face. He knew the result would be imperfect. A photo of a fax of a picture. In other words, a copy of a copy of a copy.

When he realized he couldn't improve the images, he folded the fax paper and put it back under the telephone. He took a second or two to ensure that it sat in the exact position where he'd found it. Then he stood and considered what to do next — to guarantee that he wouldn't be caught up in the murder as a conspirator or some other felony.

For a moment he imagined the telephone was a time machine. He knew he had to pick up the phone and call the police. Knew that he'd wait here for them to arrive and what he would say. Then he would be subjected to a long line of questions and he would have to explain himself. His circumstances. His motivation and innocence. The only unanswered question was, when would he initiate this series of pre-destined events?

Right now, he finally decided. Just get it over with. From his shirt pocket he drew the business card that Detective Staimer had given him that morning. He sat at the table next to the phone, called into Central Station and within a minute was connected to Staimer.

After he made the first call, he dialed the number to his apartment phone. After six rings the answering machine clicked in.

"Hi Cecily, it's me." He realized that his voice was a mere whisper. He cleared his throat and tried again. "Look, something's come up on this story I've been working on. The *Post* has hired me. Good huh?" He injected a note of pride into his voice. "But the story's much bigger than I thought. *Much* bigger." He paused and decided that was all she needed to know for now. "I'm pretty sure that I'll have to go back to Central Station for another talk with the cops. Call Bisk and tell him what's happening. Tell him to be on-call in case I need him. I'll be home as soon as I can after that." He considered how to finish. "And Cecily, I'm going to need your help to do some internet research, all right? I'll give you the details later. Okay, that's it for now. I love you," he said and then added, "And the baby."

And the baby. He realized that he'd never said that he loved the baby before. Too bad it had to be like this, on a voice message.

※

61

D. F. Bailey

After he hung up he heard the radio play the whining guitar solo from Neil Young's *Southern Man.* Funny, Will thought, for the past ten minutes he'd blotted out the continuous stream of rock from the boombox. All he could hear was the sound of his thoughts. And his heart pounding.

He stood at the bathroom door and gazed into the living room. For a moment he considered turning off the music, but he knew that Staimer would reproach him for messing with the crime scene. He suspected he had only a few minutes before the police and the forensics team arrived. He drew his camera from his pocket and began to photograph every item that could provide a lead to Seamus's killer.

He took a photograph of the phone faceplate that showed Seamus's number under the plastic veneer. He then captured a series of random images of everything scattered on the table. A dozen samba CDs. A soft pack of Marlboro cigarettes, half-empty. A copper ashtray brimming with inch-long butts. A deck of matches from a club called Burley's. The current edition of *Entrepreneur* magazine. Perhaps Seamus had been considering a new line of business, Finch thought. Something to diversify away from child prostitution, blackmail, and murder.

He turned to the TV stand. Beside the three clickers neatly aligned side-by-side, lay a soft sleeve nylon laptop case. Empty. Finch took a picture of the case and a close-up of the embossed brand on the cover. *Lenovo ThinkPad.*

When he heard the heavy knocking at the door, he slipped the camera back into his courier bag and called out. "Just a sec."

"Open up, Finch."

He recognized Staimer's voice and turned the lock on the door. Behind Staimer stood a uniformed cop and two others carrying mobile forensic duffel bags. The detective studied Finch for a moment. He shook his head as if he couldn't quite believe he was encountering him for the second time in one day.

"Good. At least you've got gloves on." He pushed past Finch and quickly assessed the room.

"In there," Finch said and pointed to the bedroom door.

Staimer stuck his head into the bedroom and then swung back toward his colleagues. A look of dread knit across his face.

"It's bad," he said with a brisk nod to the forensic team. "I'm going to call in the LT." He pointed to the man in uniform, "Oberon, guard the door. Nobody gets inside, understand?"

Oberon clenched his jaw, nodded his assent and stepped back into the hallway.

Staimer paused as if he'd just discovered something unusual. "Jackson, turn off the damn stereo, would ya."

Staimer turned to Finch again.

"Did you touch anything?"

Will had to think a moment. "The doorknob." He made a gesture to show that he'd been circumspect.

Staimer eyed him with a grimace of disdain. "What else?"

"The phone." He pointed to the landline on the table.

"You can't use your own phone?"

"Don't have one."

Staimer blinked in surprise. "So, no phone. Who'd you

call?"

"You." He shrugged. "And my fiancée. Told her I was going to be late tonight."

"I guess you are." Staimer's temperament seemed to mellow.

Finch offered him a weak smile.

"That's it?"

"Yes."

The music from the boom box cut to silence. At once, Finch felt as if a measure of sanity had been restored to the crime scene.

"All right. You wait outside with Oberon. Then I'm taking you back downtown for another talk. Your chair's probably still warm from this morning's visit."

CHAPTER EIGHT

"OKAY, FINCH, TELL me how you found Seamus Henman." Detective Staimer's eyes narrowed to thin slits as he leaned across the table.

They sat in the same room they'd occupied earlier that morning. Room 3. Nothing had changed. The ceiling camera, the steel table, the chairs, the claustrophobic atmosphere. They sat in the same positions with Finch facing the mirrored, one-way window. If anything had changed, it was Finch's increased sense of doubt and anxiety. He decided to tell his story from beginning to end without embellishments.

"It was pretty straightforward," he began, "I went to Henman's place on Cesar Chavez and knocked on the door. There was no answer so —"

"Stop." Staimer held up his hand as if he might be bringing a line of traffic to a halt. "What the hell did you think you were doing there?"

"My job. I'm covering this story for the *Post.*"

"What?" A flash of astonishment crossed Staimer's face. "This morning you were an impoverished student at Berkeley. Now you work for the *Post?*"

Finch chuckled at that. He could imagine Staimer's surprise. "Yeah. As of this morning." He reached into his bag, retrieved the envelope containing his freelance contract and passed it to the detective.

Staimer pulled a pair of reading glasses from his shirt pocket and studied the contract for a few seconds. "You mind if I make a copy of this?"

Finch pondered proposition. "To be honest, yes." He knew he needed to be cautious. "Look, don't get me wrong. I'm cooperating with your investigation. I'll tell you whatever I can to help. What happened to Seamus Henman is sick and whoever knifed him has to be put away" — he waved a hand in the air — "but I'm not going to add to the file you already have on me."

"No? I can arrest you for unlawful entry into Henman's apartment right now." Staimer's voice grew more shrill with every word. "Then you can explain all this to a judge. Would you prefer that?"

Finch blinked. Point taken. "All right. But I want the original."

Staimer frowned and left the interview room with the contract dangling from his hand. Less than five minutes later he returned.

"Here you go. The *original* is yours." Staimer slipped his glasses into his pocket, folded the contract into its envelope and passed it back to Finch. "Let's go on from where we left off. So how did you get Henman's address?"

"From Jojo."

"Jojo?" He tapped a fingernail on the metal table top that

separated them. "This morning I asked what else you knew. And you neglected to tell me this? His address?"

"No." Finch glanced away to diffuse the tension. "I didn't know it then. She told me this afternoon."

"You saw Jojo this afternoon?"

Finch wondered how to explain the brief meeting with Jojo and Biscombe. "Look, I helped her find a lawyer. I brought him down here to your meet-n-greet cage. After I introduced them, she told me about Henman and his address."

"What was the lawyer's name?"

"John Biscombe."

"Spell it."

Staimer put on his glasses again and wrote the name on a pad as Finch spelled it out. He also took down the lawyer's phone number and slipped the pad back into his pocket. A moment of silence slipped between them, then Staimer's demeanor changed. His face soured as if he'd been cheated. Finch knew that he would have spent hours trying to pry See-See's address from her. Obviously, he'd failed.

"Shit, you are in so far over your head. You know that?" He pressed his lips together and glanced away as if he'd lost track of what to say next. "You don't even know which way is up, do you?"

"I think so." He pointed his index finger to the ceiling.

Staimer sneered with a pish of disgust. "All right, what else did she tell you?"

"She told me where he kept his apartment key."

"Go on."

"Which was on the door sill." He made a sweeping motion

D. F. Bailey

with his hand above his head as if he were grabbing the key.

"Then what happened?"

Finch revealed the details of his exploration of Henman's apartment beginning with hearing the music, the overflowing ashtrays, the stink of rotting meat. Then he described finding the corpse and everything that followed up to the moment when Staimer arrived at the apartment. The one detail he omitted to disclose was the series of photographs he'd taken with his camera. That was part of his reporting and none of Staimer's business.

"All right, Finch. I'm going to have to talk to Jojo again and this lawyer of yours." His attitude had returned to a more neutral, professional tone. He stood up. "I want you to stay here until I'm done with that, and then —"

He was interrupted by a heavy knock on the door. Staimer pulled it open and stepped into the corridor. With the door ajar, Finch could hear a brief, whispered conversation that ended with a curse. Then Staimer returned to the interview room, shrugged and said, "I could see this coming from a thousand miles away.

"Looks like your evening shift is only beginning, Finch. The feds just pulled this case from my hands. You've got another meeting about to take place down at FBI regional headquarters."

"The FBI?"

A hint of sympathy emerged on the detective's lips. "I wish you luck. I mean it."

Finch felt a shudder roll through his belly. Where could this be headed?

"Do me a favor, would you?"

"What's that?"

"Call the lawyer. Biscombe. And my editor at the *Post,*" he added. "Wally Gimbel. His number's on the freelance contract."

Staimer examined him with amusement.

"Tell them to meet me wherever the feds are taking me." When Staimer failed to reply, Finch implored him. "Look, can you help me out with this?"

Staimer nodded once, a bare acknowledgment. "All right. I'll do what I can."

※

The FBI office in San Francisco was located above the court-house in the Phillip Burton Building on Golden Gate Avenue. Like a lot of federal buildings, the tower — a twenty-one story hive constructed of concrete, steel, and glass — was devoid of personality. We might as well be in Moscow, Finch thought as he traveled up the elevator with Agents Busby and Albescu. Busby sported a brush cut and appeared to be in his early fifties. He had a thick body and the lumbering gait of a long-retired wrestler. Albescu was maybe forty-five, taller, leaner, and his face conveyed a worn, depleted energy.

By the time he stepped into the Bureau's premises on the thirteenth floor, over two hours had passed since Detective Staimer had left Will on his own in Room 3 at SFPD's Central Station. The delay extended past the dinner date he'd made with Cecily. No one provided an explanation or apology. However, Finch was grateful for the lapse because when he entered the FBI's office complex, he discovered Wally Gimbel standing beside John Biscombe beneath the EXIT sign at the far end of the corridor. His detainment had provided enough time for his allies to assemble. The two men appeared to be engaged in a quiet conversation. As they spoke, Wally turned the brim of his gray Fedora hat in his hand.

Finch turned to Busby and Albescu and tipped his head toward his colleagues. "Give me a minute, will you. I've got to talk to my lawyer."

"Bisk, good to see you!" Finch marched over to his friend and shook his hand. He turned to face his editor. "Wally, sorry to drag you in here. Especially at this time of night. I wasn't —"

"I told you to keep me up to date," Wally held up a hand as he interrupted Finch. "I just didn't expect that we'd do the de-brief here." He smiled with a reassuring grin that set Will at ease.

"Look," Finch said. "This thing is now a double murder. Seamus Henman has been killed. It looks like some kind of psycho wack-job."

"What?" Wally's question came out in a whisper.

Finch knew he had to be succinct. "I'll tell you everything later. For now, I want you to take my camera. I don't know if they're going to arrest me and I don't want this to fall into their hands."

Wally nodded mutely as Finch drew the camera from his pocket and placed it in Wally's hand. The editor slipped it into his suit pocket and unbuttoned his jacket to ease the slight bulge.

"And Bisk, just keep me out of jail, all right." He eyed his friend with an intense stare. "And if they do bust me, let Cecily know everything's okay."

Biscombe nodded. "Just don't lie to them. They can lock you up for that alone."

The three men turned when Busby called Finch's name.

"All right," Finch said. "Don't hesitate to step in whenever you can."

The FBI interview room was much more comfortable than the SFPD's Room 3. In fact, Finch soon realized that it was a staff meeting room furnished with swivel chairs that surrounded an oak table. A glass wall opened onto an wide space equipped with about twenty workstations, each endowed with computers, telephones, and more swivel chairs. Apart from three other agents typing on their keyboards, their war room was vacant. Given the hour, Finch was not surprised.

"All right, let's start." Busby sat at the head of the rectangular table. "I'm Agent Dan Busby. This is Agent Raymond Albescu." Busby tipped his hand toward his colleague. "Now I understand that you two are here at the request of Mr. Finch. Please introduce yourselves."

Will smiled at the overt formality. Busby spoke as if Miss Manners herself had raised him. However, beneath the polished veneer, Finch detected a no-nonsense rigor and discipline. He knew he had to be careful, or this meeting would destroy his career before it began.

Wally and Biscombe introduced themselves and their professional capacities. Then Busby nodded at Albescu, who spoke in an almost tender voice that belied the long-suffering expression in his face.

"I want to reassure you that, at present, no one here is currently under suspicion of any crime. However, we'll be recording the meeting." Albescu pointed to a voice recorder in the middle of the table. "We're investigating the murder of Seamus Henman which was reported to us this evening." He set his eyes on Will. "Apparently you called it into the SFPD sometime after six o'clock, is that correct?"

Aware that it was his turn to reply, Finch nodded.

"For the microphone, please," Busby said and pointed to the recorder.

"Yes." Finch felt his voice catch in his throat. "It was six-forty-seven."

"How did you know the time?" Albescu asked.

"From the clock in the bedroom."

"Do you know if the clock was accurate?"

"What?"

"Was it fast or slow?"

"No. I don't know." Finch shrugged. Fast or slow? He thought Albescu was attempting to discredit him with this question. His tone suggested he was pulling rank to let Finch know that he was a mere cog in the investigative wheel that was about to grind him to a pulp.

As he'd done with Detective Staimer, Will walked the two agents along with Biscombe and Wally through the details of the two murders. However, neither Busby or Albescu expressed any interest in the death of Gio Esposito. Perhaps they believed it was a suicide. But when he described the situation in Seamus Henman's apartment, they forced Finch back and forth through the particulars three or four times.

Where did he find the key? What was the music playing on the stereo? Were windows open or closed? What did he touch besides the telephone? What food was left to rot in the kitchen?

After a pause, the agents exchanged a glance. Finch detected a change in their body language. A slight shift that suggested they were prepared to interrogate him about something more important.

"Let's talk about Henman." Albescu spoke in his foggy voice. "What did you notice about his body?"

"You mean the knives? That he was strapped into the chair?"

"Both. Tell us what you remember."

"Well, he was strapped with duct tape to a wooden armchair by his ankles and wrists. And his mouth was taped shut, too." That was the easy part. Finch blinked as he recalled the mental notes he'd made as he'd taken one picture after another. "I saw a serrated knife had penetrated his right ribs," he continued. He drew a long breath and pressed on. "There was a wide blade, like a meat cleaver, in the stomach. Then a carving knife buried in his upper left ribs that probably went into his heart." He blinked again as if he could dismiss each image in turn simply by shutting his eyes. "A filleting knife had cut across his throat from left to right. Then it was stuck in place below his right jaw." He paused again to regain some composure. "Finally, I saw a short paring knife buried in the left ear."

"Jeezus," Biscombe whispered under his breath.

Busby exchanged a nod with Albescu. Finch had precisely recalled the types and the positions of the knives, and the demeanor of the body. Other than providing the clinical details, it was unlikely the forensics unit would add much more in their deposition about the corpse.

"Give us a minute," Busby said and signaled Albescu to follow him outside the interview room. They stood and moved into the central office. Busby closed the door behind him, and the two agents turned to the left and walked out of Finch's view.

"My God. I can't believe you were there." Biscombe folded his fingers into a fist and pressed them to his mouth.

Wally ignored the lawyer and turned to Finch. He tipped his head toward the digital recorder to remind him that they were still being monitored. With a flick of his wrist, he tossed his Fedora hat over the machine. It landed with a flop, completely covering the device. Then he shielded his mouth with a hand and leaned in towards Finch and Biscombe.

"Now listen, Will. Something's gone south on these guys. I can tell they've been caught with their pants down on this. Right now, they're trying to sort out a deal they can agree on. I don't know what it is, but in any case, it will give us a bargaining position. I want you to let me handle that part, okay?"

Finch nodded.

"Does the camera have pictures of the body?"

"Yes. Everything."

"Good. Unless they ask, don't say a word about them."

"Wait a sec." Biscombe held up a hand. "If you conceal pictures you took, you could be charged with withholding evidence of a crime."

"That's debatable," Wally said with a shake of his head. "The camera doesn't hold any evidence the forensics teams won't get on their own."

Biscombe's face bore some skepticism. "You asked me to keep you out of jail, Will. So, I'm cautioning you. It's risky."

Finch considered his options. He drew a breath and said, "I'll keep the camera undisclosed. For now."

"All right, my friend."

"Okay." Wally turned to the lawyer. "John, once we start negotiating I'm going to bring up our first amendment rights. When I do that, I want you to hammer them with some legal bafflegab. Got it?"

Biscombe nodded. "Don't worry," he said. "I'm with you on this."

"All right." Wally pulled his hat from the recorder and set it back on the chair beside him.

When the two FBI agents returned to the meeting room, they both studied Finch with a determined glare. They sat in their chairs and set their forearms on the table. Busby, the veteran, spoke first.

"What are your intentions on reporting all this?"

Wally leaned forward, his expression calm and relaxed. He waved a hand to shift their attention to him. "I've told him I want the full story on my desk for tomorrow's edition."

Busby paused before he continued. "I'm sorry, but we can't allow that."

"Can't *allow* it?" Wally laughed heartily. "Last I checked, we can print whatever we want."

Busby shook his head. "Not in this case."

"This case?" Wally's eyebrows arched below his forehead in a gesture that said, tell me more.

"Until we've done a complete investigation, the details of Seamus Henman's murder cannot be publicly disclosed."

"So what is it about Henman that can't be disclosed?" Wally said, his voice friendly, dismissive of their objections. "The actual fact of his murder?"

"No. You can report that."

Wally smiled with a warmth that embraced this first, small concession. "Or, our belief that he's tied to the death of Gio Esposito?"

"That's a speculation you can make," Busby allowed, "but unless you can prove it, you could soon be arguing that in court."

Wally nodded. "Ah. So then it's this business about the five knives, isn't it?"

Busby waited before he responded. "Yeah. That's off limits."

"Well, I'm sorry," Wally continued, his voice growing firmer with every word, "but our first amendment rights allow us to inform the public of the details and circumstances of Seamus Henman's murder."

"And you *know* that," Biscombe said with authority — and on cue. "You may be the FBI, but Thomas Jefferson and the founding fathers had no intention of ceding freedom of the press to anyone."

"Oh, spare me." Busby laughed with disbelief and then glared at Biscombe in silence. After a moment he looked at Albescu, who nodded and then turned to Wally. "Look — and this is all off the record — we have a national investigation underway that concerns public safety. Until we get the forensic reports on Henman and determine how it affects our on-going investigation, we ask you to hold back the details of the stabbing. The five knives as you call it."

"For how long?"

Busby glanced at Albescu. "Three working days?"

Albescu said, "Yeah, that should do it. That'd take us to next Monday."

"And what do we get in exchange?" Wally asked.

Busby shook his head in a fatigued manner. "What do you want?"

"An exclusive interview with the *Post* when the case is closing." Wally spoke with the self-assurance of a pro. Now that they'd reached this point, it seemed as if he'd been steering toward a bargain since he'd entered the room. He was ready to close. "And one, or both of you, will do an exclusive interview with Will Finch at least one hour before the FBI goes public with this case."

Again Busby and Albescu consulted with a single look followed by a nod of agreement.

"Deal."

※

When they stepped onto the sidewalk outside the Burton building, Wally led Finch and Biscombe to the corner of Turk Street and Larkin. The night traffic shunted through the intersection in fits and starts. With the background noise no one would overhear them. Wally took command of the conversation.

"Okay, first things first." Wally adjusted his hat to deflect the light rain from his face. "Will, you need to duplicate whatever's on the camera and store it in a safe place. Can you do that?"

"I think so."

"Think so?" he said with a frown. "That's not good enough."

"After you dupe it, I'll take the copy," Biscombe offered. "I've got a secure system set up in my office."

"All right." Wally nodded and passed the camera to Finch who slid it into his courier bag. "Now let's deal with the case itself. We need to be first to report this thing. Like I said to Albescu and Busby, I want the story on my desk by noon tomorrow. Can you deliver?"

Finch took a moment to assess his situation. He felt tired and hungry. He needed to bring Cecily on board. Her internet research skills would be critical. She could access over a dozen national databases through her account in the library. That would help. He imagined a series of steps leading the way forward. First, deal with the camera. Then ask Cecily to help him. Then grab some food. Then he'd write a first draft. Then sleep. Tomorrow morning when she went to work, he'd wrap up the story and email it to Wally.

"Yeah," he said. "That won't be a problem."

"Good." Wally smiled broadly. Apparently, he was warming to his new freelancer. "Now look, from what I can see, there're two stories here. And Jojo is the link that joins them. If the story grows legs, you may have to interview her again. Where is she?"

"Lock up," Biscombe said. He checked his watch. "Just about this time tomorrow they'll have to charge her or let her go."

Wally raised his eyebrows with a cynical frown. "If they let her go she'll disappear. Can you keep an eye on her?"

"I'll see what I can do," Biscombe said, resigned to the fact that Jojo had now risen to the top of his very short client list.

"Good." Wally turned back to Finch. "Meanwhile I'm going to assign Olivia Simmons to research any other murders resembling the five knives. That's the only reason the FBI is blocking us. Maybe the perp's a serial killer. Who knows?"

A moment of doubt caught Finch by surprise. He'd already concluded that Henman's killer was disturbed. But a serial killer? Worse, however, was the feeling that he'd lost control of the story. He didn't want to surrender any part of it to another writer. Wally recognized his concern and made a gesture of conciliation.

"Remember, this story started with Olivia. Unless it's a clear stand-alone story, you'll share the byline on anything you write together. And vice versa."

Finch started to protest, but Wally interjected.

"Will, you're part of a team. So play like it." He pinched his thick lips together to signal the end of the discussion. "Email me your story by noon tomorrow. And I'll want an update from you by six tomorrow evening."

"All right." He shifted his head from side to side as he contemplated the new assignment. "You got it."

Without another word, Wally Gimbel swung about and marched down Larkin Street toward the Civic Center Garage. The drizzle shifted to a steady rain, and Finch pulled the hoodie over his head. He turned in the direction of the BART station on Market Street, and Biscombe followed along beside him.

D. F. Bailey

"What do they say in journalism? The story has legs?"

"Yeah." Finch chuckled. "That's what they say."

"Well, this sucker is turning out to be a foot-long centipede. Better watch, those things can bite."

Finch steered them under the overhead awning of a jewelry store. The rain came down with a force that caused the canvas to pool above them. They paused to wait out the worst of it. After a few minutes, the fury seemed to subside.

"You ready to move on?" Finch asked.

"Sure. Let's go."

As they continued, Finch felt a measure of relief. It felt good to have Biscombe at his side and Cecily at home. He embraced the assurance of Wally's guiding hand and the certainty he possessed. The old man had managed to negotiate a compromise with the FBI — something that Will knew he could never handle on his own. And while the problems in the story were growing more numerous and more complex, he now believed that he could solve them. Most of them, anyway.

CHAPTER NINE

AFTER WILL DUPLICATED the SD card from his camera and gave the copy to Biscombe for safekeeping, he made his way back to his apartment in Berkeley. When he opened the door, he saw Cecily standing next to the little table overlooking the rain-soaked street. He'd now broken two dinner dates in a row, and he didn't know what to expect.

He shook the rain from his jacket and hung it on the coat peg next to the door. Then he slipped to her side and kissed her. She kissed him back and wove her arms over his shoulders.

"It must have been a bad day," she whispered. "Bisk told me about some of it. You all right?"

"Bad and good. I'll tell you about it later." He pulled back a little to examine her face. She had a Mediterranean complexion, olive skin, and dark hair that fell in thick curls past her neck. She rolled her soft, full lips together and kissed him once more.

"Look, I'm sorry I missed our dinner. Again," he said.

"No worries. Besides I had to compile a last-minute inventory report for Shirley," she said. "But I got roti take-out from JotMahal. It's ready whenever you want to eat."

JotMahal. His favorite. Over the past six months, he'd developed a fondness for Indian cuisine. A sense of gratitude swept through him. He'd stood her up two days in a row, yet she didn't reveal a hint of irritation. She was a wonderful woman, and he knew he was lucky to have her.

"How's the baby?" His right hand swept over her breasts and down to her stomach. She wasn't showing yet. They were only ten weeks in.

"I saw the heart beating today!" Her voice rose with a sense of wonder.

"You did?"

"Yeah. At the clinic. You want to see the video?" She teased him by stroking his right earlobe with her fingers.

"Yes."

"You sure?"

"Of course!" He knew she was toying with him. It was a good game, tender and intimate. "Can you tell if it's a boy or girl?"

"No, silly. I told you. Not until eighteen weeks."

"Eighteen?" He knew about the eighteen weeks, but he wanted to prolong the idle chatter that came with her pregnancy. It was so new to both of them. "Okay, so show me."

Over the next half hour, they watched the fifteen-second clip of the baby's heart beating on the computer monitor while they enjoyed their flatbread rolls. Will drank a bottle of IPA, but Cecily had gone off alcohol the same afternoon that she told him she was pregnant.

After they ate, Will related the events of his day, beginning with the triumph of landing a freelance contract at the *Post*.

Their celebratory mood shifted when he mentioned the corpse he'd found in Seamus's apartment. He kept the details to himself, but let her know that the murder was brutal enough to bring the FBI into the case — which led to his evening interview with them.

Because of his increasing anxieties about the two deaths, he avoided any description of the homicide. With the baby on the way, he knew Cecily didn't want to hear any of it. Besides, she'd seen her share of misery over the past five years. She'd proven herself to be strong enough when she dealt with the death of her brother. Then came her parents' divorce. No, he decided to save the nitty-gritty facts of the grisly murders for the story he planned to write later in the evening.

"Any other news?" he asked.

"Yeah. Alison agreed to come to the wedding. As my bridesmaid."

He smiled. There'd been some question of her family members getting involved. Her mother would come. Now her sister. Perhaps her father would make his way down from Seattle to join them.

"That's a step closer. Looks like you might have a family reunion after all. Perfect for Thanksgiving weekend."

"Maybe." Her lips flattened into a pout. "I feel a little sad that you won't have anyone."

"Don't be. You know I've been on my own for five years now." He paused to recalculate. The year after his father died, the year he'd finished college, he'd enlisted in the army. Four years of service and two more here at Berkeley. "Make that six years."

"Yeah. Well, pretty soon that's all going to change." Her eyes brightened. "Then you won't be alone anymore. Think you can adapt?"

He laughed. "Oh, I can adapt all right. How about we roll into the bedroom. Then I'll show you how adaptable I can be."

"Uh-huh?" She laughed and let him draw her into his arms. "Maybe I should call you flexible Finch."

"Maybe you should." He started to kiss her neck. "Let me know what you think in half an hour."

※

After they made love, Finch forced himself to climb out of the bed. He knew that if he fell asleep with Cecily in his arms, his writing plan would fail. He checked the digital clock on the kitchen stove. 12:17. He decided to write until two-thirty, then crawl back into bed. Cecily usually left for the campus library around eight-thirty. If he got up with her, he could start the second draft by nine and meet Wally's noon deadline.

Before he began to write, he pulled the Canon Powershot from his courier bag and reviewed the series of photographs he'd taken over the past twenty-four hours. It was a chronicle of everything that led him to the horror in Seamus Henman's apartment. But of all the pictures on the camera, the innocuous images he found in Gio Esposito's office drew his attention. The shot of Esposito holding the catfish against the Ozark Lake pier measuring post showed that he stood at least six feet tall. And probably weighed close to two-fifty. How did Seamus Henman, a scrawny welterweight, manage to throw Esposito through the apartment window?

Then he noticed the picture of the telephone on Esposito's

desk. The ten phone numbers captured in the screen memory display. This was something that Cecily could track down. She had access to a reverse-call directory in the Berkeley library. Type in a number, out comes a name and address. One of the perks of her job. More than once she'd tracked down up-to-date information he needed for his journalism research. She'd been a big help to him. Now he needed her support more than ever.

As he wrote the telephone numbers on a sheet of paper, he realized that two of them were repeat calls, which meant Esposito had spoken with only eight individuals. When she woke up, he'd give her the list and see what she could dig up. Satisfied that he had enough material to work with, he turned his attention to drafting the news story.

He opened a new file on his laptop and began to type. As Wally suggested, the story hinged on Jojo's connection to Esposito and Henman. He would start with her.

Police are investigating two deaths related to Joanne Joleena who was found handcuffed half-naked to a bed in an apartment in Chinatown on Monday night.

Gio Esposito, an investment advisor who fell to his death from the apartment on Washington Street, was an acquaintance of Seamus Henman. Henman himself was found dead in his Mission apartment yesterday afternoon.

Joleena, who worked for Henman, said that he arranged their meeting with Esposito. Joleena has been detained for questioning by police.

Apart from confirming both deaths, the SFPD has not

D. F. Bailey

revealed details of either investigation. However, in an exclusive interview with the Post, *Joleena claims to have been duped into a blackmail scheme designed by Henman to pressure Esposito.*

He reread the opening. The first two paragraphs were vital. He knew he'd written a decent lead and he could shape the story from that foundation. He decided to reserve the details surrounding Jojo's bondage for the end of the story. A blatant tease to draw readers into reading the entire article. And he wouldn't disappoint them. But the facts he had about the two murders were most important. They provided the nuts and bolts of the crimes, and he would lay them out first. From there the story would build to a disturbing conclusion: San Francisco had a killer on the loose.

Who was he and where would he strike next?

CHAPTER TEN

FINCH WOKE WITH a start. He felt something sweep through the room and out the door. Was it a ghost or a shadow? Then he realized he was at home. But that meant the phantom was — *where?* He heard Cecily brewing coffee in the kitchen. Fully awake now, he tried to shake the apparition from his head. During his tours in Afghanistan and Iraq, he'd encountered more than a few soldiers who confessed to believing in ghosts. While their beliefs may have been delusions, the soldiers' fear was real.

Before Cecily left for work, Will gave her the list of eight phone numbers to track down. Then he showered, dressed, and ate the bacon, eggs and toast that she'd set aside for him. After breakfast, he drank two cups of coffee and re-drafted the story he'd written the night before. When the article reached the point where any new changes tended to sacrifice precision and clarity, he closed the file and attached it to an email that he sent to Wally Gimbel at the *Post*. It was eleven-fifteen. The story was in before the deadline. To the best of his knowledge, it was accurate — but obviously incomplete. If anything, it would leave his editor wanting more.

He smiled at that. Yesterday Wally had come to his defense against Busby and Albescu, the two FBI agents. Compared to the mixed reception he'd had from Wally before he'd signed the freelance contract, now the old man seemed to appreciate the risk Finch took when he entered Seamus Henman's apartment. Good, he said to himself. Give me a chance, and there'll be more of that coming your way.

As he washed the dishes from last night's roti feast, he considered his next moves. First, he wanted to interview Jojo again. Wally suggested that she might reveal something new. Had she been arrested and kept in lock-up in Central Station, or had the SFPD released her without charges? John Biscombe could tell him.

Second, he wanted to talk to Olivia Simmons. Wally assigned her to research the background to Henman's murder. The five knives. Had anyone else been killed with the same, exacting inhumanity? Hopefully, she'd discover some leads to move that part of the story forward.

He placed the clean forks and knives in the cutlery drawer, and a new thought came to him. Baghdad in 2004. He'd caught wind of a similar murder using multiple knives. He'd been ordered to investigate the story and called one of the officers in the 49th Military Police Brigade, Jeremiah Rickets. He'd talked about it with J.R., who at the time, denied the rumors. "Never happened," J.R. had insisted. That afternoon Finch filed a NAR — No Action Required — report to his CO and put the story out of his mind. But now, here it was again. Could it be?

He pulled the balcony curtains to one side and gazed at the steady rain slapping against the asphalt. He planned to take a

BART train down to Market Street and walk to the *Post* editorial office on Mission. He grabbed an umbrella from the hall closet, slipped his courier bag over his shoulder and pulled the hoodie over his head. Ready for another day on the front lines.

Twenty minutes later he boarded a car on the westbound line. As the train rumbled from Ashby to West Oakland station, he studied two men in their mid-thirties standing next to the door. One tall, one short. One shaved bald, the other brimming with curls. They were engaged in an intense but private conversation. When the train rolled into West Oakland, the car door slid open, and the men disappeared into the crowd of exiting passengers.

Like ghosts, he thought. Then his dream returned. The phantoms fleeing before him. But now he could see them slipping through the open door. Finally, it all made sense. There was Gio Esposito, the six-footer holding a twenty-pound catfish from one hand. And Seamus Henman, the peewee lightweight, bound to a chair with duct tape and left to bleed out in his bedroom. A total mismatch. Seamus Henman didn't throw Esposito from the eleventh floor window. He could never have managed it. A second man had helped him, someone with enough heft and grit to throw Esposito to his death. Someone capable of slicing and dicing Seamus Henman the next day.

※

Will tossed his courier bag beside the empty desk and settled into the swivel chair. The *Post* newsroom hummed with a quiet buzz as a dozen reporters typed at their computers or spoke on their telephones. He liked the mood and energy — a hive of intelligence, discipline, and common purpose. As he observed them, he felt at home. This was a place where he could begin a new life. More than that, it was a place where he could thrive.

As Olivia Simmons slipped down the aisle of desks, he broke from his reverie. She appeared to recognize him.

"Mr. Finch. Back for more punishment?"

Her voice carried a light-hearted lilt. Hopefully, she didn't harbor any resentment against him for scooping her story. She sat down and set her purse, a black leather handbag, on her desk. She wore a gray blouse buttoned up to the throat, a tan vest and black dress pants that bore a sharp crease on each leg. She struck him as professional and experienced — an appearance that made Finch feel like a novice. Suddenly aware of his jeans and leather jacket and the hoodie that draped over his neck, he pulled off the jacket and fleece to reveal his clean shirt with a button-down collar. He smiled.

"Can't keep myself away," he said to try to engage her. Besides, it was true. He considered what Wally had told him yesterday. Be a team player. That meant making amends. "Look. I think I should apologize for being a little abrupt yesterday."

She turned her chair toward him. "You *think* you should, or you're actually going to apologize?" She raised an eyebrow with an expectant air.

He chuckled to himself. Obviously, she wanted to enjoy the moment of his repentance.

"Going to." He put on a grin. "I mean … this is me, apologizing right now."

She replied with a half-smile, more like a pout, he thought, but enough of a gesture to suggest he'd won a pardon.

"Okay, let's get to work," she said. "Wally asked me to follow up on this five knives thing." She studied him a moment. Her irreverent tone had vanished. "I heard that you were in his apartment. That you saw what happened to Seamus Henman."

"Yeah."

"Wow." Her eyebrows arched with bewilderment. "That's brutal."

He tipped his head to one side and nodded. Then he asked, "So did you manage to dig anything up?"

"Mmm-hmm. Have a look." She opened a file folder on her desk and waved him over. "Two stories. One from the *Wichita Eagle,* the other from the *Reno Gazette-Journal.* The first story came out in April this year. The other in July."

He rolled his chair next to her and glanced at the photocopied pages without reading the stories. "So one in Kansas, another in Nevada. And now California. Each attack just three or four months apart."

She shrugged off the notion that the sequence could be meaningful. "People sometimes look for patterns where none exist. Their first mistake is to make assumptions from a data set that's too small."

"Right. And three's too small."

"Way too small."

He nodded in agreement. "Maybe we'll find more important info from the two articles. Similarities, idiosyncrasies, that kind of thing. Can I borrow them for a while?"

"Of course. Another point to remember is that if the FBI believes there's a serial murder spree underway, it's likely they'd only acknowledge the bare facts. Until they solve it. Then they'll want to hit the front pages with all the gory details."

"You mean there might be five or ten murders out there with the same MO — the five knives — and nobody knows it?"

"Or more. And some of *them* could be copy-cats." She shrugged as if the possibilities were unlimited.

He rolled his chair back to his desk and began to read the story from the *Wichita Eagle*. Again the memory of his brief investigation of the rumored knife killing in Iraq crossed his mind. For the first time since he'd returned to America from his deployment, he felt the cold snake of war coiling at his feet. He could almost hear it, too. The hissing.

※

Finch read the article from the *Wichita Eagle* through once and then pulled his notebook from his courier bag and made a bullet list of what he considered the pertinent points.

- *The victim, George Sculley, a white male in his mid-forties, lived alone in his second-floor apartment.*
- *Sculley was unemployed, "known to police," but had no criminal record.*
- *The police reported that he'd died of five discrete knife wounds. Five knives were buried in his stomach, ribs, heart, throat and one ear.*
- *None of his neighbors reported any sound of disturbance other than a rock 'n' roll station playing through the night of the murder.*

- *Neighbors called Sculley "quiet," "not a problem," "a guy who kept to himself."*

The apparent similarities to Henman's murder struck Will immediately. The knives, the music, the loner. He realized he needed to check if Henman had a previous record. If he'd been pimping teenage girls for very long, the answer was probably a yes. Biscombe could determine that. Also, he made a note of the reporter on the Wichita story: Barry Doe. He knew he should call Doe to see if the local police had requested that he suppress any details which could further identify the nature of the crime.

Then he turned to the second article in the *Reno Gazette-Journal*. The reporter, Jane Cojocaru, had written a mere sketch of the crime compared to what Doe had written three months earlier. Perhaps the FBI had jumped on Cojocaru before she could break the story. Why not? That's what they'd done to Finch. Nonetheless, he made a second bullet list based on her reporting of the murder in Reno.

- *The victim, Jerome Bartleby, a single white male, thirty-three, had one previous conviction for possession of a controlled substance.*
- *Lived alone in a downtown apartment. Over a six-month period held and lost three jobs in the kitchens of various local restaurants.*
- *Police reported that he'd been found bound to a chair and died of five knife wounds to different — unspecified — parts of his torso and head.*

D. F. Bailey

Finch then considered the similarities of the two victims to Seamus Henman's murder. The five knives, of course. And all were single white males. If Henman was known to police, then all three of them dropped into the same kettle of fish. The differences? The background music in one, but not reported in the other. One bound to a chair, the other with no mention of restraints. One unemployed, the other couldn't hold down a job.

On a separate sheet of paper in his notebook, he started a To-Do list. He identified the tasks that he had to complete to make more sense of the story.

1. *Talk to Jojo. Did she see a third man?*
2. *Henman — did he have a record?*
3. *Call Barry Doe — Wichita story.*
4. *Call Jane Cojocaru — Reno. Story squashed by FBI?*
5. *Reconcile similarities / differences: Wichita vs. Reno.*
6. *Talk to Jeremiah Rickets: 5 knives in Baghdad?*

He stopped there. Then he drew connecting arrows from item one to item six. Contacting Jeremiah Rickets was now job one. If he could link the rumors in Iraq to the Henman and Esposito murders, everything would change. And if he could make a compelling argument to Wally Gimbel by six o'clock, he knew the story would jump to the front page.

※

As Finch pushed through the door on Guerrero Street and

stepped into the 500 Club, he imagined that Jeremiah Rickets had anticipated Will's arrival seconds before he entered the bar. It was a personal quality Finch grew to appreciate after working with Rickets for six months in Baghdad. Something he'd never encountered in anyone else: this uncanny ability to predict what people might do or where they might suddenly appear. Or how events might unfold when layers of cause and effect multiplied to produce battlefield surprises. This extraordinary skill or talent — combat clairvoyance or whatever it was — had proved its merits in several situations in Iraq. Rickets became a favorite companion of soldiers horrified by the IEDs that littered the roadways in and out of the Iraqi capital. Improvised Explosive Devices could tear off an arm or a leg. Or kill you straight out. But Rickets just danced past them all.

"Stick to J.R. like black on a bruise," the survivors had advised the new joes. *Black on a bruise* became a mantra to anyone who'd witnessed Rickets's magic on patrol.

But for the mojo to work, they had to call him J.R. Jeremiah Rickets hated his name. Loathed *Jeremiah* — "too Biblical" he'd confessed to Finch once they could trust one another. He despised *Jerry* even more. ("A minor cartoon character and a yuppie comedian.") Worst of all was his surname: "a bone disease." So you either called him J.R. or you stood outside his circle of protection.

Finch recalled all this as The 500 Club bartender pulled a draft of pale ale for him. From a distance Finch nodded to J.R. and then wandered over to his corner table. They traded a fist bump and a thumbs-up handshake.

"Good to see you, man." Finch sat and sipped the foam off the top of his ale.

"Wish I could say the same." J.R. wiped a hand under his nose and glanced away as if he were blocking a sneeze.

"What? You expecting some trouble?" Finch's voice held a note of wariness.

"Well, when you called and asked me about the five knives...." He let this idea hang and then added, "What did you expect? I'm telling you there's nothing but trouble back there. And I don't want any part of it."

Finch settled in his chair and studied J.R. for a moment. A scrap of beard covered his square jaw. His teeth were yellow. The once tight, black skin on his face had become thick and puffy. Finch wondered if he'd found sanctuary in steroids of some kind. It had been two years since he'd last seen him, years that had not been kind to the thirty-year-old from South Chicago who'd joined the 49th Military Police Brigade after his first tour in Baghdad. J.R. had won two medals and been promoted up the ranks twice. But whatever pride he once bore had faded.

Will set his forearms on the table and leaned forward. "So you're saying the five knives thing is true. It *did* happen in Iraq."

JR's head flicked to one side as if he'd taken a slight nudge to the jaw. "Yeah. It wasn't just rumint," he allowed.

Rumint. Rumor and intelligence. Finch recalled the group-speak that evolved among the troops in Iraq. His favorite turn of phrase was the "self-licking ice cream cone." A reference to an operation launched to serve its own political ends. Which was almost all of them. Evidently part of J.R. still inhabited that world. At least in his mind.

"I was never sure," Finch said. "When I was ordered to track it down in oh-four, no one would step up and confirm or deny it."

"Yeah, well. Like so much else, they kept it deniable. Not like that shit storm you found at Abu Ghraib. When those photos came out? The Hajji prisoners stripped naked, chained up, dogs at their balls." He looked Finch directly in the eyes. "That was you, wasn't it?"

Finch frowned and turned away. "Still can't talk about that, J.R. I thought you, of all people, would've figured that out."

J.R. chuckled and took a long drink of beer. "What I figured out back then was that you were way more than a power-point ranger."

Finch laughed at the jibe. He'd been called a flak and a desk jockey. Powerpoint ranger was new to him. Yeah, J.R. was still living back in the sandbox.

"What I know now," he continued, "is that you were in Military Intelligence. They put you into Abu Ghraib undercover. To try to contain it. But when *60 Minutes* spilled the beans, that meant someone leaked the story. That was you, wasn't it?"

J.R. was close. Too close. "And you know this — *how?*"

He smiled again. J.R. seemed almost happy now. He tapped two fingers to his left temple. "Black on a bruise, man."

"Lucky for me that won't hold up in court." Finch winked at him, a signal that while J.R. might be closing the corner on what actually happened at Ghraib, it was time to move on. He glanced away and then turned his gaze back to his friend.

"So … the five knives. Did you personally see any victims?"

J.R. set his elbows on the table and bunched his hands together in front of his mouth. He blinked — a slow, heavy motion of his eyelids. "Twice."

"So there were two victims."

His eyes narrowed. "More."

When he realized they were talking in whispers, Finch leaned forward. "How many are we talking about?"

"At least four. That's the number of official sheets I read."

"You think there could be more?"

"Fuck, it was the sandbox, man." His voice rose with an edge of anger. "You know that. Some of them prob'ly just sank under the moon dust."

"Yeah. I know." Finch leaned back in his chair to consider this. He needed just one or two more answers, and he could wrap this up. "Did you ever find who was doing it?"

"Who do *you* think it was?"

"I don't know. A psycho. Special Ops. Meat Eaters. That's why I'm asking you. That was *your* patrol with the 49th Brigade."

"Yeah, that was my unit all right." J.R. shook his head from side to side, a gesture that he had nothing more to add. "I ask you about Abu Ghraib, and you lock the door. Now you want me to dish details on the worst thing I seen over there? It's tit for tat, man. Show me yours, and I'll show you mine."

J.R. frowned, fed-up with the interrogation. Finch knew that he was likely to balk at any more questions. He decided to change direction.

"All right. So look. Now he's showed up here."

"Who?"

"The killer. The five knives."

"Here?" J.R. glanced around the room, a mock grin on his face. "Where's here, man? Frisco?"

"Maybe." Finch knew that he couldn't reveal too much detail. It would be a violation of his deal with the feds to mention the killings in Kansas and Nevada.

"What's that mean?"

"It means … I think so. Maybe," he said again, an attempt to backtrack.

J.R. shook his head with a weary despondency.

"Look, after hearing nothing from you in what — two years? — you phone me today, ask to meet here in my neighborhood bar. For what? To walk down memory lane with an old army joe? No." J.R. dropped his hands onto the table, palms down. "Why? Because you got a new job on a paper and now you need some intel. And don't get me wrong, that's good for you. *Good* for you. Every one of us could use a new job. Hell, I just *lost* my job working in security. Had it for six months, then poof. Vaporized." He snapped his fingers and stared at Finch with a gesture of helplessness.

"Geez, J.R. Sorry to hear that." Will leaned back in the chair, wondering what more he could add. "I mean it."

"Look, you have to understand — this is *painful*. Man, it hurts me to tell you all this shit."

Finch watched the emotions stream over JR's face. The story had opened something in him that Finch had never seen before. Under the thin veneer of J.R.'s military bravado lived a man struggling to contain the horror of what he'd seen in the war.

"By the way, this is *so* you," he continued. "You know you're the only friend I have like you — and I got plenty. Black, white, Asians. Girls, men, and women. You're the only one who never opened your door to me. Not a crack. That's what made you perfect for Intelligence, I guess. You never show your cards, man. That's good for poker. But in life? That just makes you sad and lonely."

Finch nodded. He knew that J.R. had it right. At least partly. He'd wanted to tell him about Cecily. About the baby. But a wariness kept him buttoned up. Especially around J.R. who could intuit almost anything tucked below the surface.

"You're right. I know it." He leaned forward again. "Maybe because I felt some fear."

"Fear. What are you afraid of? Me?"

"I don't know." He shook his head and shrugged. In fact, J.R. did frighten him. Talking to him about their time in Iraq brought the horror back into own his life, too. Better to make a joke about it. "Or maybe it's like you say. I really am sad and lonely." He added a weak laugh.

J.R. rolled his lips in a frown. "Well, that's something. Not much. But at least you tossed out a crumb."

He drank off the dregs of his beer and pulled a gray watch cap from his jacket pocket and tugged it over his head. "Okay. I gotta go."

Finch checked his wristwatch. "Me too. J.R., look, I know what you're thinking about all this. But if something new breaks on this story can I call you?"

"I don't know." He rubbed a hand over his jaw as if he were searching for an honest answer. "What for? I just told you all I know."

"In case something comes up that I need to double check." Finch remained in his chair. He had a feeling that J.R. wanted to leave the 500 Club on his own.

J.R. pulled a jacket over his shoulders and shook his head. "It's not a good idea, Finch. It brings back memories, man. I just can't go back there anymore."

Finch watched him amble toward the front door. J.R. waved a hand to the bartender but didn't turn back toward Finch. Then he pushed through the door, stepped into the rain and was gone.

CHAPTER ELEVEN

"HEY BISK, IT'S Will calling."

"What, you got a new phone?"

Finch coughed up a weak laugh. "Very funny. No, I'm calling from the *Post*. Look, I need to track down Jojo. When I called Central Station, they told me you were on hand when they released her."

"Yeah. First thing this morning." Biscombe drew a long breath. "You know she's only seventeen, right? Legally, still a child."

"Seventeen going on twenty-two. A dangerous age if you ask me."

"No doubt about that. I met with her social worker, and she's gone back to her group home. Did you know about her parents?"

"What about them?"

"Both killed in a shoot-out outside a bank. Almost two years ago. An armed robbery over in Emeryville. They weren't involved, just passing by on the sidewalk in front of the bank. Hard to believe."

Finch considered this. Another horror story shatters a

young kid's life. He'd had his troubles as a teenager when his mother died. And then four years later, his father passed on. But that was nothing like Jojo's disaster. He shook his head wondering how she could move forward and find her way in the world following the murders of her parents — and now, Esposito and Henman.

"You think she'll be okay?"

"She's lucky. She's in one of the better foster homes in town. Seriously, if she's capable of getting her life in order, she's in the right place."

"Ever the optimist, Bisk. Do they teach that in Berkeley Law? Pollyanna 101?"

He chuckled at that. "Yeah, I was first in a class of two hundred."

Finch smiled, glad that he could change the mood. John Biscombe was the most upbeat person he'd ever known. Somehow law school had failed to suck the optimism out of him.

"So look, I've got two favors to ask."

"Whoa, I am *so* surprised." Biscombe's turn to serve up some sarcasm. It was a game they liked to play from time to time. Outsmart one another in exchange for a good laugh.

Finch let the derision pass. "The first is, can you check to see if Seamus Henman had a police record."

"Sure. That's easy. Makes me think you're trying to soften me up for favor number two."

"No, no. That's a gimme."

"A gimme?"

"Yeah. Can you gimme Jojo's address?"

"Ahhh. Should've seen that coming." He paused as if he

might be switching his phone to his other ear. "Hang on. I've got it somewhere ... wait a sec."

Finch could hear Biscombe shuffling some paperwork. When he found what he needed, he gave Finch an address on Euclid Avenue.

"So why do you need to see her?"

"Something new on the story. Jojo's pimp, Seamus Henman, I'm sure he couldn't have thrown Gio Esposito through that window. He was a foot shorter and a hundred pounds lighter."

"Really?"

"At least. Sure, he could push Jojo and a few other teen girls around. But not Esposito."

"So what are you thinking?"

"That a third man was in the Chinatown apartment. The guy who threw Esposito onto the street, may be the same guy who killed Henman. If that's the case, Jojo probably knows who he is."

※

Before Finch made the trek out to Jordan Park and Jojo's group home on Euclid Avenue, he borrowed a hand-held digital recorder from the *Post* receptionist. He usually relied on his notebook to record salient information, but when he needed to, he could recall exact quotes by memory alone. In fact, as a party trick, Will liked to recite memorable lines from writers and politicians, especially the one- and two-sentence barbs from Mark Twain. He could also regurgitate word-for-word zingers from Winston Churchill. His favorite was the retort to Harry Truman when the president described Churchill's successor, Clement Attlee, as "a modest sort of fellow." Churchill's reply: "He's got a lot to be modest about."

Despite his excellent memory, Will wanted to get Jojo's words formally on the record because he knew that if she revealed the name of the third man in the apartment, it could serve as evidence in court. It would also provide some protection against any defamation lawsuit that might be filed against him.

When he knocked on the door to the group home, he quickly realized that he would have to take Jojo out of the building to do a comprehensive interview. The rooms in the Victorian house were small, the walls paper-thin. Furthermore, a constant stream of teenagers rolled up and down the staircase into the kitchen, bathroom and living room.

"You again?" Jojo said as she descended the stairs to the main floor hallway.

"Surprised?" He smiled. It felt good to see her again. She rubbed a hand over her eyes and he wondered if she'd been sleeping. She wore a soft pink cotton blouse and denim jeans with parallel razor cuts at the knees. Almost like the healthy, average seventeen-year-old girl Biscombe predicted she would soon become.

"Yes and no." She waved him along the hallway. They stood at the front door. "Your friend got me out."

"I know. He was the one who told me you were here."

"I think I want to be a lawyer." She cracked a smile. "You think I can?"

Her comment took him by surprise, and he grinned. From teen hooker to attorney in forty-eight hours. "Yes. Of course. I imagine you could do just about anything you set your mind on. But how'd you decide that so fast?"

"The way he got me out." She snapped her fingers. "One day I want to do that."

He nodded, thinking, well *maybe*. She had the guts for it. And the street smarts.

"So this place doesn't look too bad." He swept a hand toward the living room. The white, lacy curtains. The plush, heavy cushions on the sofas and chairs. The brick fireplace. "Way better than I imagined."

"Yeah, except they have *rules.*"

"Everyone has rules, Jojo."

She rolled her face into a broad sneer and brushed her bangs aside. "Not like this. Curfew's at eight every night."

He shrugged, surprised that she couldn't recognize how good she had it here. There was jail or this. Pick one.

He checked his watch. Three-ten. "You hungry?"

"Starving."

She was in the mood for a burger and led Finch down to the corner of Arguello Boulevard. From there they took a right on Clement and strolled over to the corner of 2nd Avenue to a restaurant nestled under a bright red awning called EATS. A crowd of teenagers and twenty-somethings sat around the crush of tables, talking in a loud buzz above the sound of jazz samba streaming from two speakers suspended from the ceiling.

Finch found a table at the far end of the room next to the corridor that led to the washrooms. When they sat he could tell that her flippant mood had shifted to something more agreeable. Besides, she was hungry now and let him know it.

"Can I have the twin burger and a Diet Coke?" she asked.

"Sure."

"With yam fries."

He laughed at that. "If you want."

Finch ordered a cappuccino, and when Jojo's meal arrived, he studied her while he sipped his coffee. As she ate, her hair swung from side to side to cover one cheek, then the other. He noticed that her eyes had cleared, the smudged mascara washed away. Today she looked her age: seventeen. The night they met, twenty-five. Despite her shifting identity, there seemed to be something steady about her, he decided. An inner resilience. Maybe Biscombe was right. She was intense and alert; that would always be part of her. But the stress of the evening she'd spent handcuffed to the bed — and the next two days locked up in Central Station — all of that was now gone. In its place, a kind of strength welled through her.

"How are the yam fries? All right?"

"Good." She smiled a faint grin that exposed her chipped tooth. "Everyone says they're the best."

"Everyone?"

"In the group home."

"You going to be all right there?"

She offered an indifferent shrug. "Maybe. For now at least." A hesitation. "Why do you care?"

"You want the truth?"

She sipped some Diet Coke through a straw.

"Or just more BS?" He offered this as an alternative, knowing which one she'd choose.

"I heard you were the one who found See-see." She studied

him now and held his eyes without breaking away.

"You mean Seamus?"

"That's his real name? Everyone calls him See-see."

"Okay. Well" — Will drew a breath — "he's dead."

"Yeah. So I heard." She closed her eyes for a moment and considered this. "What happened to him?"

"The FBI is on it. So I can't tell you exactly."

"The FBI." She coughed up a cynical laugh. "What? They made you promise?"

"As a matter of fact, they did."

She frowned to suggest that she knew he was straying from the facts. Preparing to feed her more BS. "Look, *who* are you anyway? Why did you want to find See-see? And like, why are we even talking?"

"Fair question." He leaned forward. "I have a contract to write a story for the *San Francisco Post.* The story started with Gio Esposito, the guy who went through the window. Now it's about Seamus Henman, too."

"Henman?" She laughed as if she couldn't quite believe it. "That's See-see's last name?"

"Yeah." When he recalled she didn't know Henman's surname, he wondered if she could tell him anything useful about the third man. Mr. X. "Look, Jojo. I want to ask you a few more questions. And I want to record what we talk about."

He fished the digital recorder from his courier bag and showed it to her.

"Okay?"

She gave him an I-don't-care shrug and took another pull on the straw.

He clicked on the recorder and lay it on the tabletop between them.

"All right. I'm just going to say a few things to make sure everything's clear." He paused and smiled at her. "This is Will Finch speaking to Joanne Joleena, about the events that happened three nights ago." He stated the date and time and place where they were now talking. With the preliminaries out of the way, he leaned back a little. He smiled again.

"So, you've already told me about the night in the apartment. About Gio Esposito and then Seamus Henman, the man you call See-see. Right?"

"Yeah, so?" She slurped the last sip of Diet Coke and pushed the glass to one side and lay her hands flat on the table.

"So I want you to look at a picture of a man. I have it on my camera. I want you to tell me his name if you recognize him, okay?"

He drew the camera from his bag and took a moment to find the image of the photograph he'd taken of the fax sheet in Henman's apartment. He held the camera about a foot from her face. Her eyes dilated, and he could tell that she recognized him. The rectangular face, the ape-like ridge in his brow, the dimpled chin. She pulled the camera into her hands with a gasp.

"Where did you get that?"

"Who is he?"

She glanced away as if she was trying to clarify the image of his face from her memory.

"Where did you get it?"

"From See-See. It was in his apartment." He leaned forward. "Jojo, who is he?"

She set the camera on the table. "Felix."

"Felix who?"

"Just Felix." Her eyes seemed to study something in the distance as she tried to sort out the logical connections between the three men. "I guess See-see must of called him in."

Finch struggled to put the pieces together. "So you think Felix was there that night? In the apartment?"

A glimmer of recognition crossed her face. "Yeah. He just glanced at me from the living room. It was like, two seconds. At first, I didn't recognize him. But seeing his picture now — yeah, it was Felix." She brought Finch back into focus. "The only time anyone ever saw him was when there was trouble."

"What kind of trouble?"

"*Trouble*-trouble." She shook her head. "I mean *he* was the fucking trouble."

Finch understood now. "Jojo, this is important. What is Felix's last name?"

A flash of anger crossed her face. "How the fuck do I know? Nobody tells you their last name. All you ever get is some BS name like Jingles or See-see. Or Jojo," she added and stared at him as if she'd finally realized that her world had imploded.

The heat of her anger simmered and then seemed to vanish. Her cheeks slackened. She covered her eyes with her fingers and buried her hands under a long plume of her beautiful golden brown hair. A moment later Finch saw the tears roll down her cheeks as she sobbed quietly.

Perhaps Bisk is right, he thought. She seemed ready to get

this out of her system. To stop playing the call-girl for a string of losers and accept that she was a teenager who'd been robbed of her youth. Maybe she was ready to reclaim her life and set it back on track. And maybe one day she'd be the lady lawyer who springs underage hookers from jail. Maybe.

※

Finch returned to his desk at the *Post* just before five. Ten to fifteen reporters clicked away at their keyboards, most of them trying to hit a deadline, he figured. Olivia Simmons was not in her cubicle, but her purse was tucked under her desk, and a jacket draped over her chair.

Now that he had a first name — *Felix* — to attach to the picture on his phone, he felt the momentum of the story pick up again. He opened his laptop and started a new file. Will wanted to draft two hundred words before the six o'clock meeting with Wally. It would help if he had more information to add. Another angle. Details which showed the story had taken on a new dimension. Maybe Cecily had dug up the names corresponding to the list of telephone numbers from Gio Esposito's landline.

He called her at the Berkeley library, wondering if she'd already clocked off for the day. He felt a moment of relief when she picked up the phone on the second ring.

"Good. You're still there," he said.

"Yup. Busy day here."

"Really?" Did that mean she had no time to research the numbers?

"Uh-huh," she said. "And I can hear it in your voice."

"Hear what?"

"Your question. Did I find time to check out those phone

numbers?"

From the way her voice rose with every syllable, and the way she let the words linger, he knew that she'd done it.

"And you did, right?"

"Yes, Mr. Finch, I did," she growled. She called him Mr. Finch whenever she thought he was getting too pushy. Her way of establishing limits.

"Okay, so you're killing me here. Stop teasing and give me the names."

"Got a pen handy?"

He typed "NAME" at the top of the file on his laptop and clicked to a new line. "Okay, shoot."

"First one, Golden Boy Pizza. Second, TD Ameritrade." She read off the list of contacts. The first five were either business or fast-food calls. "Only three of the eight are connected to private numbers. Two of the three were the repeat calls you identified. Okay, so the first repeated call is to Seamus Henman."

"Seamus Henman? He's the guy I found dead yesterday." Finch blinked. "Wait a second, give me a minute to check something."

Will set the phone aside and dug his camera from his courier bag. He scrolled through images he'd taken in Henman's apartment. And there it was, a picture of Seamus Henman's telephone number under the transparent plastic cover of the phone base — an exact match to the numbers listed on Gio Esposito's phone index. How had he missed that? He could have connected Henman to Esposito yesterday. It meant that the story was running ahead of him. Or that he was running behind it. He took this as a sign that he wasn't as thorough as he should be. He chastised himself and picked up the phone handset again.

"Yeah, it's him," he said, his lips barely moving. He didn't want to explain his mistake to her. Not yet.

"Oh my God. You mean the dead guy was one of them?" Her voice gasped as if someone had nudged her away from the phone. Then she asked, "What does it mean?"

"I don't know yet." Finch felt a rush of adrenaline as he typed Henman's name. "So Seamus Henman took two calls?"

"Right. Then someone named Julian Blomquist. Also two calls."

"Okay. He's new. That's B-l-o-m-q-u-i-s-t?"

"Right."

"So who's the last one?"

"Felix Madden."

Bingo. Felix now had a last name. *Madden.* "That's M-a-d-d-e-n, right?"

"Yup, two d's. Just one call to him."

He eased back in his chair. Felix Madden. He couldn't quite believe that the man Jojo had identified from the photo had been on the phone with Gio Esposito the day before he died.

"Cecily, this is magic. Amazing that you dug this up."

"There's more."

"What kind of *more* are we talking about?"

"I did some research on these guys."

"You did?" He leaned forward again, ready to make some new notes on the laptop. "So who are they?"

"Blomquist is CEO of a company called TruForce — one

word, and no 'e' in Tru — Investments. They have an office in the Financial District. Looks like they handle portfolios of some big league investors. And their board of directors is a *Who's Who* of retired politicians and corporate types." She paused as if she might be shuffling pages of notes she'd printed out from her online research. "I can give you all this tonight if you want it."

"I do. What about the other two?"

"Seamus Henman is like the invisible man. Except for an arrest for drug possession, which I think might've been dismissed. I don't have access to criminal records. All I can search are directories, like the reverse-name database for phone numbers, and online archives from the media, mostly newspapers. Maybe Bisk can tell you."

"Maybe. I've already asked him to check it. What about Felix Madden?"

"Okay, so you need to be careful with him." She hesitated again. "He's had a couple of convictions. The *Post* archives show that he's done jail time in Ironwood Prison. Ten years ago he was front-page material. You're not going to interview him are you?"

"I don't know." He considered the possibility.

"The guy is real trouble."

Exactly what Jojo had said. "If I do, I won't go alone."

"You promise?"

He nodded to himself, thinking, yeah, you can't jeopardize anything. Not when she's having a baby. "Of course. I promise."

He paused as he pondered one last question.

"Look. I've also got a fax number. I should have given it to you with the others. Can you look it up in your reverse directory?"

"I think so."

"You got it in front of you?"

"Yes. Shoot."

Finch gave her the number at the bottom of the fax he'd found under Henman's telephone — the fax containing the image that Jojo had identified as Felix. He waited while Cecily ran the number through the database.

"So here's a coincidence," she said.

"Let me guess," he said. "It's from TruForce Investments."

"No. It's from Blomquist's home on California Street. I think it's an address in Nob Hill."

"Blomquist. Again. That's three hits from him."

"The research on him is puzzling. It's like he suddenly appeared in 1998. Nothing before that."

Finch shrugged. "Well, the internet was just getting underway in the nineties. Google didn't even launch until ninety-eight. Maybe the system just hasn't caught up to his early life yet."

"Maybe." She seemed doubtful.

"I can't believe you dug all this up." He felt as though a dozen pieces of the jigsaw puzzle had suddenly clicked into place. "Thanks. I mean it."

"Sure." Her voice sounded dismissive as if she did this sort of thing all the time. "I handled it on my lunch break."

"No lunch? Okay, that settles it. I'm taking you out for double sushi."

"Good. I'm starving."

Her voice sounded breathy, almost romantic — and it aroused a feeling in him. Then he checked his watch.

"Okay, but … whoa, not tonight. I've got a meeting with Wally in twenty minutes."

"Who's Wally?"

"Gimbel. My editor."

"In other words, your boss." She sighed. "So that definitely means no dinner."

"You're right. Not tonight, anyway. So," he said, "can we do another rain check on that?"

※

Finch nailed down a hundred and fifty words on his new story before Olivia Simmons dug him out of his cubicle.

"Wally was expecting you five minutes ago," she said. An irritated frown crossed her face as she wrapped her arms in a knot across her chest.

"Sorry. I had to print this before I see him." He shoved his laptop into his bag and waved a sheet of paper from one hand. "You in on the meeting, too?"

"Yes." She led the way through the warren of cubicles, "the bog" as she called it. "And I've got something you should hear."

"Like what?"

"Tell you later." Olivia opened the door to Wally's office and waved Finch ahead of her.

Wally glanced up from his computer. His eyes had a brooding expression. "You're late."

"Sorry." He waited a moment, knowing that missing a

deadline of any kind was a form of negligence. "But I think you'll understand when you read this." He passed the paper to Wally and sat in the same chair he'd occupied on Tuesday when Wally dismissed his freelance proposal. The editor had changed his mind then. Maybe he'd be flexible today, too.

Olivia sat beside him, and they exchanged a glance. She radiated an aura of disdain. But beneath that, he could feel some personal warmth from her. It was a mix of emotions that he couldn't quite decode. As Wally read the article, Finch decided to let her stew.

"So you think the story has legs. It's got up off the floor and started to run a marathon." He passed the paper to Olivia and turned his attention to Will. "You're saying Gio Esposito's death is tied to Seamus Henman's murder. And that an ex-con, Felix Madden, killed them both. And both murders are tied to Julian Blomquist. *Really?*"

The skepticism in Wally's voice made Finch hesitate. "I think so." He shook his head. Then he leaned forward. "I mean, I'm *sure* of it."

"Julian Blomquist. You know *who he is?*"

Before he could reply, Olivia set the sheet of paper on the desk and sighed with exasperation. "We can't print this. We'll be sued as soon as the paper hits the street. We need a second source on every one of these allegations." She pointed a finger at the story as if she couldn't believe it was under consideration.

Wally settled her down with a nod. Be patient.

"He's the CEO of TruForce Investments," Finch said. "A hub of California wheelers and dealers. Look, the reason this story seems so *big,* is because it's so *bad. "*

Wally paused for a moment.

"All right. So spell this out for us. There're five or six moving pieces to this thing, and I want to see how the wheels align before we print a word." He tipped his head forward to suggest Finch had one chance. Now or never.

"Can I use the whiteboard?"

"Be my guest." He rolled his right hand toward the rectangular white board bolted to the wall.

Wally and Olivia turned in their chairs as Finch eased past them to the far end of the oak table. He took a blue marker in his left hand and studied the blank space before him. His head nodded up and down in barely visible ticks. Then he wrote three names in the center of the board, one on top of the other: *Joanne Joleena, Gio Esposito, Seamus Henman.* He drew a circle around the names. To the left of the circle he wrote *Pushed,* and below that, *5 Knives.* To the right, *TruForce / Blomquist.* Above the ring he wrote *10 Phone Calls.* Below it, *Felix Madden (Photo).*

"Let's start with what we know." He drew a breath. "Gio Esposito, owner of a one-man business called Esposito & Associates, bundled scores of mortgages together into stock packages called Mortgage Backed Securities. MBSs. He created two or three of these things a month. Simply roped them together — on paper, at least — for his chief client, TruForce Investments."

He drew a line of dots connecting Esposito to Blomquist. "What's the value of these things? Well, depends who you talk to."

He stopped to glance at Olivia.

"Olivia and I both interviewed Adrian Shouldice, a mortgage broker who shared Esposito's office. He says MBSs sell for billions around the world. But now they're swirling around the toilet. You know who agrees with him?"

Finch paused to watch Wally offer an empty shrug.

"Warren Buffet. And guess what? This past summer, France's biggest bank, BNP Paribas, refused to deal with any more MBSs."

Finch turned away from the whiteboard and then circled back. "So Blomquist, looking ahead, knows Esposito's securities will soon be worthless. He wants his money back before the market crashes. He threatens to ruin Esposito. How? Sexual blackmail. He hires Seamus Henman to videotape Esposito with Joanne Joleena, a seventeen-year-old foster child, half-naked and handcuffed to a bed."

He ran a hand under his chin while he studied the board. "But then something went wrong with Henman's setup — what, I don't know yet — and Esposito was thrown through the window." With the marker he tracked a line of dots between Gio Esposito's name and the word *Pushed*. "But here's the thing. There's no way, on his own, that Henman could push Esposito to his death. Esposito was a six-foot, two-hundred-fifty-pound fisherman from Missouri. Henman was a lightweight teen-girl pimp. And smart enough to know he needed extra muscle for this play. So he goes back to the boss who arranged the blackmail sting. Julian Blomquist. And who does Blomquist recommend? Felix Madden."

While Wally and Olivia absorbed the growing complexity

of the conspiracy, Finch added a series of dots that linked Henman's name to Blomquist. And another line connecting Madden to Blomquist.

"How do we know this?" Finch's voice rose with a rhetorical flourish. "Because Henman's and Blomquist's numbers both appear in Gio Esposito's telephone call list. *Twice.*"

Finch drew arrows from Blomquist and Henman to *10 Phone Calls,* then paused to lift his camera from his bag. He took a moment to find the images of the phone numbers, passed it to Wally and then continued.

"There's more. Scroll past the telephone numbers on the camera, and you'll see a picture of Felix Madden. It's from a fax that I found under Henman's telephone. And the originating fax number?" — he drew another line of dots linking Henman to Blomquist — "Blomquist's home fax machine in Nob Hill."

Wally studied the images on the camera. "How can we be certain this is a picture of Felix Madden?"

"Because I interviewed Jojo again this afternoon. After the SFPD released her from custody, she was a little more inclined to talk to me. I've got the interview recorded."

He pulled the digital recorder from his pocket and set it on Wally's desk. Wally frowned at the device and nudged it aside. "I'll listen to it later. Just tell me what's missing."

"What's missing?"

"There's always something missing. Something you don't know. The Donald Rumsfeld conundrum: 'Known unknowns. Unknown unknowns.' What is it this time?"

Finch blinked, wondered what to add. Maybe if Jeremiah

Rickets agreed to go on record, he could reveal the possible link to the killer in Iraq. But J.R. had rejected that idea and walked out on Will. Finch decided not to mention J.R. Then another problem occurred to him. "Esposito's computer. I found printer and ethernet cables in his office, but no laptop."

"His computer. Of course." Wally rolled his eyes as if he expected this. "What about the five knives?" He pointed to the whiteboard. "The FBI is investigating Henman's link to a ritualistic killer. But now you're suggesting Madden killed him, instead."

"Maybe," Olivia said. This was the first word she'd spoken in five minutes. "I called the reporters in Wichita and Reno this afternoon. Just to see if they'd cough up anything they couldn't print in their papers."

"Really?" Finch's face revealed his surprise. Calling the reporters was on *his* to-do list. Maybe this was the "something" she mentioned on the way into Wally's office.

"Both of them hesitated. They'd been pressured by the FBI, too. And both of them refused to go on record with me. But apparently, the knife killings in Wichita and Reno were more savage than what happened to Henman. Much more." She tipped her head toward the whiteboard. "The Reno and Wichita victims' hands and feet were severed." She paused and then added, "And their genitals too."

A moment of silence weighed upon them. Finch decided that now was the time to mention his interview with J.R. "There's one more thing," he began. "I talked to a vet I knew in Iraq. In oh-four he investigated a similar set of knife killings in Baghdad. I don't know if he's the same psycho or not. My guy didn't mention anything about amputated body parts. The problem is, he won't go on record. In fact, I doubt he'll even talk to me again."

A puzzled frown crossed Wally's face. "Why not?"

"PTSD. He's got a bad case of it."

Wally shook his head. His face revealed that he was all too familiar with the ravages of post-traumatic stress disorder. "Okay," he whispered as he stared at the top of his desk. He turned his attention to Finch. "When you found Henman. Was he intact?"

"Yeah. At least his hands and feet were." Finch shrugged to suggest that he hadn't checked Henman's genitals.

Wally took a long look at Olivia. "And the reporters in Wichita and Reno? Both reported the same thing? Independently?"

"Yes. And they've never talked to one another, either."

Wally took another moment to consider her statement. Then he said, "And to you this means … what?"

"Could mean a copy-cat." She tilted her head with a skeptical air. "Could mean more than that. If Madden killed Henman to eliminate a witness, it would make a clever head-fake. Make the cops believe Henman's the victim of a serial killer. And that the Esposito and Henman murders aren't related."

"A head-fake." Wally spit up an empty laugh. "All right, all right, all right. I've had enough." He waved a hand dismissively and anchored his elbows on the table. "Okay, this is what we do. Going forward, you two are working this together." He set his eyes on Finch. "Will, do you get that? *Together.*"

"Yes. I get it." Finch could feel the adrenaline rising in his body. He walked past the whiteboard and forced himself to sit in his chair.

"I want hard copies of this fax with Felix Madden and the telephone numbers you found on Henman's office phone. Can you do that?"

"No problem."

"Good. Now, this story that you wrote" — he waved the sheet of paper in the air and set it back on the table — "needs a complete re-write. This girl, Jojo, is no longer the lynchpin. Julian Blomquist is. Olivia, I want you to fact-check every word. And remember, we can't mention the actual five knives until our deal with the FBI expires on Monday. Okay, anything else?"

Olivia raised a hand. "The apartment. It appears to be rented by a Raymond Smith. Which happens to be his real name. I spoke to him on the phone. He said that since the police talked to him, he won't go on record about anything. But when I asked him if he knew Seamus Henman, he swore at me and hung up."

"Ha-ha." Wally grinned. "So you got a four-letter-word confirmation."

She nodded.

"All right, keep that for background." He turned to Finch and pointed at the story he'd written. "I want the new story on my desk by seven AM."

"Right."

"Then tomorrow we" — Wally waved a hand across the desk — "go to meet Julian Blomquist. We show him the mug shot of Madden he faxed to Henman. The list of phone numbers. *And* the front page story you are about to write. Then we offer him a chance to comment before we publish."

"Both of us?" Will asked.

Wally frowned, worried that Finch still hadn't embraced the concept of the editorial team. "No. All *three* of us." Then he added, "And it'll be a business meeting. So if you own a jacket and tie, throw them on, would you?"

Finch shifted in his seat.

"Okay, that's it for now. Go get a sandwich or some coffee. Then call your loved ones to advise them you'll be working late."

Finch rolled his shoulders. He could see the battle coming. He felt ready for it. The good fight.

※

Will placed the latte and shrimp salad on Olivia's desk and set the black Americano and burrito next to his telephone. While he'd made the food run, Olivia familiarized herself with the material evidence Finch had gathered on his camera.

"These pictures from Henman's apartment, they're just…."

She couldn't finish her sentence. He understood. Since he'd duplicated the files and given the copies to John Biscombe, he'd tried to forget the stark images of Henman's corpse. But they still haunted him.

"The knives? I know," he said. He took a sip of coffee and unwrapped the top half of his burrito. "I haven't been able to look at them again. Fact is, it's hard to shake them from my head. It's like things I saw in Iraq."

"So you were there. In Iraq?"

He nodded. Since he'd already revealed this during the

meeting with Wally, it seemed like an odd question. But he knew that some people took offense to the war — and to anyone who'd taken up the cause.

She studied him a moment and then turned away. She pushed a pair of earbuds into her ears and inserted the jack into the digital recorder. When she found the recording of his interview with Jojo, she paused to dig a fork from the bottom drawer in her desk, unraveled the plastic wrap from her salad and began to eat. From time to time she stopped the recording to scratch a few words on her notepad and then pressed on.

Meanwhile, Finch opened a new story file. Start from scratch, he told himself, and he made a numbered list of the essential story elements.

1. *Esposito sold millions in MBSs to Blomquist*
2. *MBSs are collapsing on global markets*
3. *On record: Jojo said Henman set Esposito up for blackmail. She was the bait.*
4. *Henman had a photo of Madden faxed to him from Blomquist.*
5. *On record: Jojo identified Felix Madden in the apartment the night Esposito went through the window.*
6. *Esposito's phone shows two calls each to Blomquist and Henman, one to Madden.*

These were the bare-bone facts. Will decided to state things plainly. Make no accusations. No allegations. Let the reader join the dots. Then see how Blomquist responds tomorrow when they confront him.

After Olivia listened to the interview with Jojo, she put away the earbuds and turned to Finch.

"Wow. This's something, Will." She scooped the last leaf of lettuce into her mouth. "The photos, the recording. The DA's team is gonna drool when they see it."

"You think so?" He tucked the last wedge of the burrito into his mouth.

"Yeah. And I've got to say, Jojo is … well." She patted her lips with a napkin. "She reminds me of myself."

"How's that?"

"I know a little bit about foster homes. More than, actually."

He finished chewing, waited for her to continue.

"Let's just say, some girls make it. And some don't." Her face showed that she could reveal a lot more about her past, but she decided to keep it to herself for now.

"The lawyer on this case, John Biscombe, he thinks Jojo can make it."

"I hope so. I like her. At least the way she talks." She shoved the empty salad plate aside and took a sip of coffee. "Okay, so can I recommend how we do this?"

"Shoot."

"You start the main story. From the top, except this time work Blomquist into the lead. Meanwhile, I'm going to write two sidebars. First, what we know about the key players. Then another one on Mortgage-Backed Securities. Nobody gets them. MBSs — *what are they?* My boyfriend says they're starting to wreck the stock market. That it's already happening."

My boyfriend. Finch was glad to hear it. But he wondered about her affinity for Jojo. Had Olivia come up through a foster home somewhere? And from there worked herself onto the crime beat at the *Post?* If yes, then there was a lot more to her than he'd imagined.

"Okay. Let's do it that way," he said and smiled to himself. Here you are, pal. A team player on the *San Francisco Post.* The biggest story of the year in your lap. He turned his attention to his keyboard and began to type. An hour later he had the story nailed down tight.

A fax transmission from the home of Julian Blomquist, CEO of TruForce Investments, was discovered near the mutilated body of Seamus Henman in his Mission apartment on Tuesday evening.

The fax contained a photograph of Felix Madden, convicted of two assault charges and accessory to manslaughter in 1997. On January 15 of this year, he was discharged from Ironwood Prison.

According to Joanne Joleena, a witness interrogated by police following the death of Gio Esposito, Madden and Henman were present when Esposito fell from the eleventh floor of a Chinatown apartment on Monday night.

The partially-clad Joleena had been handcuffed to a bed in the apartment as part of an attempt to blackmail Esposito. She claims the blackmail was intended to force Esposito to refund the financial losses of TruForce Investments. She also confirmed the identity of Madden on the fax transmission.

The digital record of Esposito's telephone calls from his

office reveals that he had multiple phone conversations with both Blomquist and Henman in the days before his death.

Over the past year, Esposito packaged and sold a series of Mortgage Backed Securities (MBSs) to TruForce. MBSs are speculative investments sold for billions of dollars in North America, Europe, and Asia. Once dubbed "financial weapons of mass destruction" by Warren Buffett, MBSs have recently suffered significant losses that pared their value to a fraction of their initial prices.

Police investigations are ongoing. A formal statement concerning Henman's death is expected next Monday.

CHAPTER TWELVE

FINCH SET HIS laptop on the breakfast table and settled into the wooden chair that overlooked his apartment parking lot. For the past few days, laden with rain and fog, the window provided a dreary view. But on evenings like this, the outside world completely vanished in the ink of night. The bleak outlook suited his mood, and he prepared to spend two or three hours digging up what he could about Julian Blomquist.

Before he began to work, he took a moment to consider what Cecily had told him before she'd climbed into bed. She'd spent some time that afternoon researching Blomquist and his business from her computer in the Berkeley library.

"There's plenty of info on the internet about Julian Blomquist," she'd said as she leaned over his shoulder and started a Google search. "Most of it's about his company. But TruForce Investments started in ninety-nine. Of course, before that there's nothing. But the odd thing is, there's no reference to Julian himself before ninety-eight. None. It's like he didn't exist a day before June 13, that year. Then on June 14, he appears out of nowhere."

"Like magic," Finch said.

She raised her eyebrows with a skeptical weariness. "You figure it out. I've got a breakfast meeting at seven-thirty." She kissed him on the forehead and made her way to bed.

Now Will began a new internet search on his own. He typed "JULIAN BLOMQUIST" into the search bar and watched the results cascade down his screen. The file count showed thirty-eight pages. There were articles, pictures, interviews, magazine profiles and TV videos that went back almost a decade. All of them revealed the phenomenal growth of his financial empire — an enterprise that seemed pre-ordained for success.

Finch considered the options and then clicked on a random link. It showed Blomquist teeing off from the eighteenth tee at the Half Moon Bay Golf Links. With him were the CEOs of Ameritrade, Fox Films, and DiskMagik Technologies. Another link revealed Blomquist addressing the annual meeting of the San Francisco Lions Club. There were hundreds more: Blomquist on a float with the mayor during the Shriners parade. Shaking hands with George W. Bush. Watching the LA Lakers with his wife while Jack Nicholson pulled a long face behind them.

After twenty minutes he realized that Cecily was correct. No references preceded June 13, 1998. The problem had nothing to do with the age of the internet or Google. The pre-'98 Blomquist archive was empty. Or maybe it didn't exist.

He decided to try a different approach. Instead of typing JULIAN BLOMQUIST into the search box, he entered his surname plus a space. Google then provided ten different next-word options: BLOMQUIST HALE, BLOMQUIST JOAN, and so on. None of these offered helpful prospects. Then he typed: BLOMQUIST A. The results were useless. But when he typed BLOMQUIST B, a set of four distinct names was generated. He followed the four links and clicked through the pages associated with each name. Again nothing. Running through each letter of the alphabet, he employed the same procedure and turned up nothing worthwhile. Until he tried BLOMQUIST P.

This time four names appeared: Paul, Peggy, Peter, Per. He clicked on the links to Paul Blomquist. Up came a page with at least twenty leads. The first of these provided a community news story from the *Santa Cruz Sentinel* dated May 14, 1974: STAR ATHLETE DIES FOLLOWING GRAD NIGHT FRACAS. Below the headline was the spitting image of a young Julian Blomquist along with two other teenagers. However, the cutline under his photo identified the first youth as Paul Blomquist. Maybe his twin, Finch thought. He brought up some of the recent pictures of Julian Blomquist and placed them side-by-side to those of Paul Blomquist.

"Will you look at that," he whispered. "Same guy." He returned to the 1974 news story and read the complete article:

Pacific Preparatory School lost one of its best and brightest last Friday night during a brawl following the senior grad night. Darrell Wiggins, 18, was found dead on the shore below the Santa Cruz Surfing Museum around 11.45 PM.

City police were called to the scene when three students separately called 9-1-1 to report a fight that had erupted on the Museum grounds overlooking the foreshore cliffs.

D. F. Bailey

"It's a tragedy to see the senior grad night end this way,"
said PPS Principal Dwayne Almont. "Our hearts go out to
Darrell's family and the entire school community. On a person-
al note, I can say that I got to know Darrell Wiggins through
coaching his baseball team going back to when he was a boy of
ten. I'd never seen a more promising athlete. And from what we
all know of his sports achievements over the past two years,
I'm sure most people would say the same."

Several senior students at the Museum were questioned at
the scene. On Saturday, two students, Wayne MacAuley and
Paul Blomquist, were taken into custody for questioning and
released on Sunday. As of yesterday, police said no charges are
pending.

A public memorial service for Darrell Wiggins will be held
at the school Wednesday, May 21, at 7.30 PM.

Will glanced away and considered the implications. Did
Julian Blomquist change his name from Paul to divert attention
from his connection to Wiggins's death? Worth checking. He
turned to another article. Then another and another. After
twenty minutes he came across this headline: SILENCE BRO-
KEN, SUICIDE PACT UNRAVELS. Below the headline sat a
picture of Blomquist sporting a mustache and goatee. The story
was a front-page feature from the digital archives of the campus newspaper at Stanford University dated January 14, 1977.
In the second paragraph, Paul Blomquist was identified as a
critical player in a pact that claimed three student lives.

"They wanted me in, and for a while, I was with them,"

132

Paul Blomquist told the Stanford Daily *after the Santa Clara Police questioned him. "But it was crazy. Who would do that? Pledge to kill themselves?"*

Police are currently withholding the names of the suicide victims, but they have revealed that two of the three were women.

Blomquist, a Stanford sophomore studying business, met members of the group last fall at the campus anarchist fair. He claims that the core membership was small. "Eight to ten people tops. Half men, half women. Some of them dropped out after Christmas break.

"That's when I realized how crazy it was. When I went home during the holidays. Then I came back to campus, and this happens one week later. Did I see it coming? Yes and no. Yes, because all three of them took this insane pledge. But no, because I didn't think any of them could go through with it. Face it. It's not so easy to kill yourself."

When asked if he took the same pledge, Blomquist said, "No way. Maybe they thought I did. In the end, I couldn't tell what any of them believed. Sometimes I didn't know myself."

Finch read the rest of the story which focused on a rising trend of student suicides across the country. It was a sad testimonial to those who couldn't find their way on college campuses where competition, loneliness, and depression took a toll.

Will kept digging. An hour later he found a story dated April 27, 1983 from the *Los Angeles Times*. The headline: COCAINE TRAFFICKING CHARGES TOSSED. This time the article revealed something new: his full name. Paul Julian

D. F. Bailey

Blomquist. Finch, now confident that he'd found the link that joined the old Blomquist to the new, leaned in to read the three-paragraph news brief.

Judge Anthony Moritz dismissed all charges against Paul Julian Blomquist and Henry James Nowakowski at the Los Angeles Superior Court on Tuesday. The trial on charges of trafficking over $300,000 worth of cocaine came to an end during its second day.

The defendants' lawyer, Jason Schneider, argued that the LAPD used false statements to obtain a warrant to enter the premises and seize the cocaine. After his deliberations, Judge Moritz agreed with the defense and dropped the charges against Blomquist and Nowakowski.

Phillip Bryce, the LA District Attorney, said he would consider appealing the judge's ruling following an investigation into the matter by the LAPD's Internal Affairs Group.

For the next ten minutes, Finch continued to search for the results of the police IAG report but found nothing. Likely the document was buried or never saw light of day because the DA determined that a new trial against Blomquist would be fruitless.

Nonetheless, Finch had what he needed. Paul Blomquist and Julian Blomquist were the same person. A sort of Jekyll and Hyde. The younger version had scraped through his early life tainted by public fights, suicide, and drug trafficking. In the late 1980s and early 90s, he'd gone to ground and transformed himself. Then, with his new name and a reputation for hard work, intelligence, and street smarts, he'd created a financial powerhouse. Astonishing.

But tomorrow it would all unravel, Finch told himself. The golden threads would fall away to expose Blomquist as a corrupt businessman and criminal mastermind.

※

Finch heard the landline phone ringing. He washed a hand over his eyes and rolled on the mattress toward the night table on his side of the bed. His fingers clawed for the handset, and in his groggy blindness he tipped over a cup of water. The plastic container rattled onto the floor and rolled against his shoes.

"Shit," he moaned and wiped the water from his hand. The phone continued to ring. He grabbed the handset and pressed it to his ear.

"Hello," he whispered.

"Will, get up."

He could barely make out John Biscombe's voice, a brittle tremor on the verge of breaking. Will covered his bare legs and chest with the bedsheets and rubbed his hand across his face.

"Something bad has happened. To Jojo."

His eyes sprung open. "What?"

"The cops just called me. She's dead."

"Dead?" He checked the time. The digital clock read 9:23. Cecily would have left for work two hours earlier.

"She's been murdered. I'm going down to Central Station now. Detective Staimer said he wants to talk to me. He knows I was there for her release yesterday."

Finch swung his legs over the bed to the floor. A thin trickle of water ran under his toes.

"Staimer?" He tried to think. The fact that Staimer drew the case meant his lieutenant had linked Jojo's death to Esposito. Maybe Henman, too. Had the FBI dropped their end of the investigation?

"Bisk, can I call you later? I've got to get down to the *Post.*"

Biscombe seemed reluctant. "Sure."

"All right, I don't know what Staimer can tell you, but try to find out how she died." He waited. "And where, okay?"

No answer. Will scanned the open closet for his button-down shirt and tie. He recalled Wally asking him to wear a tie and jacket. Try to remember to put them on, he told himself. Still no response from Bisk.

"Bisk, you there? Can you do that? Find out what happened to her?"

Biscombe wheezed as though he had to recover control of his voice. "You know," he said, "underneath it all, she was a good kid."

"Yeah. She was." Finch stood up and brushed his free hand over his eyes. "She told me she wanted to be a lawyer."

"She did?"

"Because you got her out of jail. She was pretty impressed by that."

"Well." He hesitated and then said, "Damn it. She could have made it, man."

"I guess she might have." He peered through the bedroom window. The rain continued to beat onto the street. "You were there for her, Bisk. You did what you could. Nobody could ask for more."

136

※

By the time Finch rolled into the *Post,* it was coming up to ten-thirty. He dropped his courier bag on his desk and scanned the editorial pool. The bog. A dozen reporters were working quietly at their terminals. No sign of Olivia. Just past Dixie Lindstrom's desk, Wally opened the door to his office. He set one hand on the door frame and leaned into the room. He spied Finch and waved him over.

"I don't know if you heard," Finch said as he approached, "but Jojo's been murdered."

Wally tipped his head toward his desk, a gesture to join him. "Olivia's handling it. She's gone up to the kid's group home to see if they'll tell her anything. After that, she'll run down to Central Station. Doubtful, but Detective Staimer might toss her a bone."

Finch scanned the room searching for answers. The story had run ahead of him. How did it happen? Grab a few hours sleep, and suddenly you're ten steps behind.

"Did you get my story?"

"Sit down." Wally sat in his swivel chair and pointed to one of the chairs opposite his desk.

Finch settled in the chair nearest the door. He knew something had changed. Olivia had picked up this new thread. Now Wally wanted him in a one-on-one.

"Was it okay? I mean the story. Can you use it?"

Wally chuckled with a world-weary laugh. "We'll use it. It'll be on the front page. And this morning I assigned Sumner to dig in on Blomquist and his company. With the girl dead, the story's pointing to conspiracy and murder-for-hire."

Finch felt his pulse skip. Everything had jumped into over-drive. Three reporters assigned to the case. And now the editor had kicked everything into high gear.

"So what's next?"

"I've got our appointment lined up with Julian Blomquist. He's giving us ten minutes at one-thirty. With Olivia covering Jojo's murder, it'll be just you and me."

"Ten minutes? How did you talk him into that?"

"I told him we have a story that's vital to his company. But he doesn't know what we've got. We'll take your story, the fax, the list of telephone numbers" — he lifted a manila folder in his hand and tucked it into his briefcase — "then I'll ask him to go on record. If he agrees, then you never know what door will open next. If he refuses, we print that he declined to comment. I call it death by denial."

Finch nodded.

"Glad to see you found a tie. Looks good on you." Wally smiled. "Goes nice with that jacket, too."

CHAPTER THIRTEEN

JULIAN BLOMQUIST'S LIGHT tan radiated from his face when he smiled. His crisp, white shirt collar and iron-gray hair enhanced the effect of his well-groomed executive style. He wore a navy-blue, pin-striped suit with a fluffed yellow handkerchief in the breast pocket. His tie, a dull gold color, balanced nicely with the handkerchief. His firm handshake suggested a weekly routine with a personal trainer in a private gym. His eyes were a Nordic blue. His gaze, penetrating. Taken together, he embodied a force of nature. A powerhouse.

But beneath the bright complexion, Finch detected a web of veins, fiber-thin filaments that spread from his nose towards his ears. Sign of a drinker, he thought. Likely keeps a few bottles close by. He scanned the office. Sure enough, on the far wall stood a minibar with two oak shelves holding a collection of scotch whiskeys, brandy, and cognac. Enough booze to drown the memories of his past whenever they needed to be suffocated.

He wondered what traces he could find of Blomquist's previous life. The world of Paul Blomquist. The kid associated with street fights, suicide, drug trafficking. But nothing evident appeared. No high school trophies, pictures or mementos. That wayward child had been eradicated. In his place sat a master of disguise and deception.

Opposite the bar, floor-to-ceiling windows looked onto the city's financial district. Beyond lay the Golden Gate Bridge and the rolling hills of Marin County. Even in the steady rain, the city appeared magnificent. Amazing how the view from a twenty-first story office could boost your sense of personal well-being. Sure, there might be hundreds of homeless people wandering aimlessly on the streets below. Trying to find a place in this world. Trying to find a way into the building. But from up here, you couldn't see them. They didn't exist.

"Wally, weren't you on the Rotary Club board the year after I stepped down as president?" The expression on Blomquist's face implied that he and Wally were already good friends. "What? In oh-five?"

"Close. I handled the club's United Way campaign in oh-six."

"Last year?" Blomquist's face tightened with surprise. Then a smile that suggested time was moving far too fast for anyone to keep up.

"Please. Sit." He waved a hand to the two chairs opposite his desk and sat in a high-back leather chair that exaggerated his height. "As I said on the phone, I can give you ten minutes."

"Thanks, Julian. So in the past few days, something's come up. Before we publish anything, I want to give you a chance to go on the record with your side of the story." Wally brought the briefcase onto his lap. The lock tabs snapped open, and he pulled out a manila file folder.

"My *side* of the story. What story?" A knot tightened in Blomquist's throat. He tried to laugh, but could only manage a dry cough.

"Yes." Wally slipped the folder across the desk. He smiled, an expression filled with the sadness that comes with the inevitable disclosure of hard truth. "I'm here to get you on record. For your sake. And TruForce, of course."

As Blomquist opened the folder, Finch lifted his notepad and pen from his courier bag. He tapped the RECORD button on the digital recorder and placed it on the edge of Blomquist's desk.

Blomquist gazed at the fax transmission. The picture of Felix Madden. The images showing the telephone numbers on Henman's telephone display. He put it aside and then picked up the draft of Finch's article. The bombshell. "What *is* this?" he muttered as he began to read Finch's story.

"We also have a recording of an interview with Joanne Joleena. She was present the night Gio Esposito was thrown from the apartment tower."

"Who?" Blomquist's face blanched as he continued to read. "Who the hell is Joanne Jolinqa?"

"Joleena," Wally said. "She identified Esposito, Seamus Henman, and Felix Madden. Unfortunately, she was murdered last night."

"Murdered? Who the fuck *are* they?" He shrugged. Turning to Finch, he said, "Did *you* write this shit?"

"I was there, too, Mr. Blomquist." Apart from his initial greeting, these were the first words Finch had spoken. His voice was even, steady. "I interviewed Joanne three times. I found the bodies of Gio Esposito and Seamus Henman. One pushed to his death from a eleventh-floor window on Washington Street. The other brutally murdered in his own apartment."

"What do you imagine these people have to do with *me?*" Blomquist pushed the file back towards Wally. The Maui tan disappeared beneath a blush that rose from his neck up to his ears.

"It's all in the story." Finch turned his hand to the folder. "The fax originated from your residence. And two calls are from Esposito to this office. We know that TruForce purchased multiple Mortgage Backed Securities from him. Securities that are losing value every day. The fact that he was facing imminent bankruptcy forced your hand. You decided to make a move before he could use Chapter Eleven protections to shield himself from further liabilities."

Blomquist pulled the file folder towards him again, glanced at the first page as if he might have overlooked something. He covered his mouth with a hand and glanced up at the ceiling, then nodded as if he'd reached a decision of some kind.

"There's more," Will said and waited to measure the reaction on Blomquist's face. "It's not in that article, but I know about Paul Blomquist."

"About Paul." A frown creased his lips. "And what exactly do you know about Paul?"

Finch leaned forward and lowered his voice. "About your grad night fight that led to the death of Darrell Wiggins. The triple suicide at Stanford. The drug bust in April of 1983 and the lawyer who sprung you free on a technicality."

"The law is nothing *but* technicalities." Blomquist gestured with a quick tip of his head that seemed to question Finch's accusations. Then he set both hands on the desk and edged forward, preparing to issue a firm denial. Instead, he paused, leaned back in his chair, and stood up. After another hesitation, he stepped over to the wall of glass overlooking Washington Street. He slipped his hands into his pants pockets, stared into the distance and studied the cloud formations above Marin County.

"Well, there's an answer to all of that," he said after the long pause. As he continued to face the window, his right hand began to roll some loose change in his pocket.

"What might that be?" Will asked.

"When I was twelve I got my diagnosis. It's quite a thing at that age to have your life yanked out from under your feet." He spoke in a low, confessional tone. "One day you're running around a football field scoring two touchdowns a game. Teasing a few girls. Scooping the school math prize." He glanced at Wally to see if he'd appreciate the promise of a young, white boy born into privilege. Without any acknowledgment from the editor, he turned back to the window and continued. "Two months later you're in a hospital bed, clinging to life. A series of nurses show you how to prick the tips of your fingers and test your blood three or four times a day."

"Juvenile diabetes," Wally said.

Blomquist's head nodded an affirmation as he continued to ball the coins in his pocket. "That fight with Darrell Wiggins? I was just protecting myself. The people who witnessed what happened stood up for me. All of them. Wiggins was the school bully, and everyone knew it." This time he turned to Finch. Again, his head swiveled back to the window.

"So that's why the police didn't press charges," Finch said. "From what the local press reported, the school principal didn't mention Wiggins bullying anyone."

"After a tragedy, it's a mistake to take what people say as the whole truth. Eulogies are meant to console the living. Nothing more."

"What about the three women who took their lives at Stanford. Weren't you part of that?"

Blomquist lifted his hand from his pocket and waved at Wally as if he was acknowledging a point. "Your reporter's done his research, Wally." He chuckled with a derisive laugh. "The boy's a keeper."

Wally said nothing. He and Finch waited for Blomquist to continue.

"As for the suicide pact...." He sucked in a long draught of air. It sounded like he'd just climbed a steep hill. "The truth is that I was part of it. My first time away from home, but I handled it on my own. At least I thought I did. Until I met these women. Part of me wanted to join them and just give everything up. Give in to the disease. I felt their loneliness. Their despair. It affected me. Maybe 'infected' is a better word. Have you ever felt that?"

Finch found himself wondering what it would be like. He'd had a friend in high school who'd developed type one diabetes. In his late teens, he took his own life. A drug overdose. Now Blomquist's brush with the drug trade seemed like a logical — but perverse — step forward. When you're injecting yourself with insulin several times a day, it isn't a huge leap to try something more powerful. And if you fantasize about suicide and you'd seen death close at hand, then oblivion was one short step away.

"After the court case, things changed. I'd had a taste of reality, I guess. Then the insulin medication and protocols improved. I got an insulin pump. I started to use my middle name. I moved back to San Francisco and finished my degree. Got a job in finance. Within five years I had a new life."

He paused and opened his hands in a broad sweeping motion that invited some reply. Finch and Wally stared at him, at this scant gesture intended to explain himself.

Wally put his fist to his mouth and let out a light cough that broke their silence. "Julian, I appreciate your candor. But there's a larger issue here."

"I know." Blomquist held up a hand to silence him. He turned back to his desk and stared for a long moment at the telephone. Then he picked up the handset and pressed a button. When his secretary responded he said, "Gilly cancel my two o'clock meeting and apologize to Ralph. You'll have to clear the rest of my afternoon, too. Then call Bettleson. Tell him I want him to come to the office immediately." He paused while she replied, then he continued. "No, this is a priority. Tell him it's urgent."

He examined Wally and Finch with an air of uncertain hope. "To answer your question, I have no formal response to your article." He pointed to the file folder containing the draft of Finch's story. "Print what you like. You will no matter what I say. Any future communications will come through my lawyer, Frank Bettleson."

"All right." Wally lifted the folder into his briefcase and set it on his knee. "You should know that I have to inform the police about this."

"Before you go to print?"

"As soon as we leave here."

Blomquist's stoic posture faltered, and he braced himself against the desk. Beneath the toned skin of his cheeks, Finch detected a deep wariness. The air of a condemned man who'd just heard the metallic clanking as his prison door swung open, and his name summoned by the executioner.

※

Finch and Wally sat at a table opposite the bar in Novela, an up-scale club not far from the *Post* headquarters, on Mission between Second and Third Streets. Hundreds of happy hour office workers packed the lounge, eager to kickoff their evening revelries. It reminded Finch of two or three New York City bars painted in black and white and illuminated with soft backlights. However, Novela possessed a few unique twists to distinguish it from other bistros. Overstuffed bookcases lined the walls, and the drinks bore the names of famous authors and book characters. The zebra-stripe, zigzag floor tiles created a fluid, slow-motion effect as if the room were tumbling left-to-right, back-and-forth. Finch imagined that it could be difficult to navigate his way across the floor if he had one drink too many. He resolved to limit himself to two beers. Then straight home.

"That was smart. Calling Staimer right after the meeting," Finch said after he took the first swig of his beer. Racer 5 IPA.

It tasted cool and fresh. He immediately upped his drink limit to three.

"I had to bring them into the loop," Wally said. He lifted his forearms onto the table and inched forward. He was sipping a Glenlivet 18 straight up. "If I didn't tell the police what we knew before we print, they could charge me with withholding evidence — or who knows what else. No, most days we've got to work with the cops and keep them onside. I called the FBI, too. Agent Busby. Left him a message anyway."

"What did he say?"

"Dunno." Wally shrugged. "He hasn't called back."

He pulled a hot wing from one of the two appetizer plates that he'd ordered from the kitchen. The other dish held four crab cakes. Finch took a crab cake and savored the sweet meat on his tongue. He slipped into a moment of contemplation and considered the confrontation with Blomquist.

"You know," Finch said, "when Blomquist went over to the office window? I had no idea what was coming."

"The diabetes story? Until he started talking, I didn't see it either." Wally exhaled with a light chuckle and sipped lightly on his Scotch. He had a tender way of nursing it, slowly coaxing the drink along. "But a lot of kids get hit with juvenile diabetes. Not many of them go on to serial killing."

"Probably not." Will's eyebrows rose with a doubtful expression. "But that's what I can't figure about Blomquist." He took another swallow from his beer. "How did he get from this unfortunate kid — to cold-blooded killer?"

"Maybe the unfortunate kid was also a born psychopath. Maybe that makes him twice as dangerous." Wally's voice suggested nothing but contempt. "That long tale about his so-called troubled youth? He's trying to spin us. Hoping his sad story will swing the jury before it's even selected."

"You think he's *that* manipulative."

"You bet. Blomquist is one of those guys who can dress for one part — like corporate CEO — and also play a second role that nobody sees."

"Yeah. It fits his pattern."

"What pattern?"

"His double life. Paul Blomquist, the high school kid impli-cated in a lethal street fight. The junior at Stanford involved with a suicide pact that took the lives of three girls. The dealer who dodged a drug trafficking conviction on a technicality. Take away his poor-me sob stories, and the facts remain."

Wally turned in his chair and took a moment to consider Finch. "Tell me something. How did you end up here?"

"What do you mean?" Finch shrugged, unsure how to respond. "I thought you asked me here."

"Didn't you say you did a tour in Iraq?" He studied him as though the question was obvious. "I mean, how do you get from *there* — to taking a Master of Journalism degree at Berkeley?"

"Yeah. Well." He sounded as if he'd often debated the issue and never found a wholly satisfactory answer. "It's a good question."

"So tell me. I'm giving us the rest of the afternoon off" — he caught the waiter's eye and made a circular motion with two fingers — "and buying another round."

Finch wondered where to start. "You know, after Iraq, a lot

of us were left with more than a few questions."

"I get that." Wally closed his eyes and shrugged. "I did three years in Vietnam. Sixty-nine through seventy-one."

Finch did a quick calculation. Wally appeared to be about fifty-five, sixty. In sixty-nine, he would've been in his early twenties. Roughly the same age when Finch had enlisted. Too young to be smart about it. Too stupid to know it would change him.

"And your questions had no answers, right?" Wally said.

"Not many."

"So, as I said, what's your story, Will?" Wally tipped his glass toward Finch and then took a final sip of the Scotch. The waiter set another Glenlivet and IPA on the table.

"Bottom line, Iraq was both the best thing I ever did — and the worst. I mean, it woke me up. From a dream into a nightmare."

"Really? What was the dream?"

Finch tried to explain it, to make sense of his own life. Over the next twenty minutes, he told Wally the short version. He was born in New Jersey but moved to Montreal in the 1990s with his mother and father, so that his dad could work for Westmount Gems and Jewelry. The store belonged to his maternal grandfather. Will finished high school there and managed to learn to speak French. The year he graduated, his mother died. Cancer. He moved back to New Jersey with his dad and decided to try journalism in college. Four years later, the same year he finished his BA in journalism at NYU, his father disappeared. A week later he was found dead, next to a rail line outside Jersey City. Will talked about the confusion he felt. The emotional loss and lack of direction. He knew he had to shake things up. After 9-11, the call went out. Suddenly the war in Afghanistan expanded to the war in Iraq. President Bush said, "You're either with us or against us." At the time it seemed like an actual choice that everyone had to make. "So I took a step forward," he concluded, thinking that those few words offered an explanation. "I did two years in Afghanistan and two in Iraq. And it got me un-stuck."

"Un-stuck, huh? Yeah, I guess it would do that." Wally coughed up a bleak laugh. "Tell me something. How old are you?

"Twenty-seven." Finch waited a moment, then returned the question. "How old are *you?*"

"Ha! Guess I stumbled into that one. I'm fifty-seven."

"That's thirty years."

"What?"

"Difference between us."

"I guess it is." Was he so old? He shrugged as if he wanted to change the conversation. "Have you got a wife? A kid?"

"Thanksgiving weekend, Wally. That's when I'm getting married. To Cecily Hughes."

"Really?" Wally's face brightened. His smile stretched from ear to ear. "So, next month."

"Yup. And the baby's due in May or June."

"Wow." He held up his drink, and they clinked glasses. "I wish you well. I mean it."

Finch smiled, too. It was a happy moment. He hadn't told anyone about the baby. Not even Biscombe.

"I imagine you'll be looking for a job."

"Already am."

"When do you finish at Berkeley?

"My thesis is due in December. And it's ninety-nine percent done. That's it."

"What's the thesis about?"

"I'm comparing the editorial perspectives of the media in the west to those in the Islamic world. On the issues of 9-11 and Abu Ghraib."

Wally nodded, a moment of introspection. "All right. I can't promise anything, but one of the women in editorial is pregnant, too. She just asked me for a six-month maternity leave, starting in January. So I have a hole to fill. You interested?"

"Interested?" He smiled again. "Yes. Absolutely."

"Good. Okay." Wally rocked his head from side to side as if he needed to assure himself that he'd made the right decision. "In the meantime, I want you to work with Olivia to finish off this story. And the latest chapter with Blomquist." He pointed at the table to indicate that the story sat right in front of them. "I'll extend the freelance contract to carry you to the end of December. You also have that interview with the FBI coming up. Once we clear it with them, you can report on the five knives thing, too. Would that work for you?"

Finch felt as if the universe had opened a channel that flowed directly into his being. The energy poured into him. It was clean, white, pure. The one thing that he truly wanted now stood before him. He knew it was the passageway to a new world.

"Yes," he said, trying to contain himself. "Of course."

They heard a telephone chime. Wally shrugged and dug a Nokia phone from his jacket pocket.

"Yes?" A pause. "Olivia. Hi."

He glanced away with an apologetic frown that suggested he needed to concentrate on the call. It went on for five or six minutes while Finch ate another crab cake and a hot wing. At first, Will tried to decipher the other half of the conversation, then gave up. His mind kept looping back to the job offer. At the *San Francisco Post.* Cecily would be pleased. So would her mother. All the pieces were falling into place. Magic in the air.

The call ended, and Wally struggled to turn off his phone. "That was Olivia. There's good news and bad."

"Good news first." Finch was still smiling. "My rule."

"The SFPD found something missing."

"What do you mean?"

"Remember I asked you what was missing in the case. You said, Esposito's computer. The cops found it in Blomquist's house up on Nob Hill."

Finch sat upright. "That's fantastic."

"It gets better." His smile returned. The Cheshire cat grin. "A confidential source says Felix Madden's prints were found on the laptop."

"Olivia got all this?"

"Yeah." Wally's face bore a self-satisfied grin. "She's *that* good."

Finch felt his pulse quicken as the news set in. Another piece had clicked into place. He felt everything coming at him in waves as if he sat at an intersection of luck and good fortune.

"Wally, this isn't just *good* news. Hell, it's a two-point

conversion in overtime. Esposito, Madden, Blomquist. All tied in a bow." He started to think through the implications. "Madden must have broken into Esposito's office the day after he fell from the window. He took the computer and passed it on to Blomquist. That must be what Blomquist wanted all along. To get the files from the MBSs that he'd purchased from Esposito."

"Maybe."

"That would explain why Esposito's office was unlocked when I tried the door. He must have been in there just before I arrived."

"It was unlocked?"

"Yes." The second unlocked door. The troubling coincidence led Finch to realize something else. "And that's why the apartment door was open on the eleventh floor. After Esposito went out the window, Henman panicked. He realized he'd be next. He tore out of the room, and Madden chased after him. That left Jojo in the room on her own."

"Right. Jojo." Wally's voice dropped a note. He paused as a feeling of dread swept through him. "Olivia caught some new info on Jojo, I'm afraid. This is where the bad news comes in."

For a moment Will froze. "So where did they find her?"

"Under some shrubs over in The Presidio."

"Some shrubs. How did she...?" Will couldn't finish his question.

Wally raised two fingers and made a slicing motion across his neck. He glanced away. "Sorry. I know you got to know her pretty well. It happens sometimes."

Finch couldn't respond. He thought of Biscombe. The cops

D. F. Bailey

had called him about Jojo that morning. Then he was supposed to contact Finch, but he'd never heard back from him.

"I wish I could change it...." Wally was still talking, but Finch missed most of what he'd said.

"Sorry. I need a minute."

"I understand." Wally threw back the last of his scotch, his slow, steady drinking pace now breaking out in a sprint. He draped his raincoat across his arm and stood up. He checked his watch. "Five-fifty. I've got to get back to the office to handle some of this. But you take the rest of the night off. Tell Cecily the news about your job. I'll cover the tab."

"You sure?"

"Yeah. Besides, Olivia's staying late." He rolled two hot wings in a paper napkin, then he wrapped the bundle in a second napkin and shoved them into his pocket.

"Can you be in at seven tomorrow morning?"

"You bet." Finch drank the last of his second beer and stood up. He felt steady now. Good that he'd kept it to two only.

"And something to keep in mind going forward." He lifted his briefcase in his free hand.

"What's that?"

"It might not feel like it yet, but this is a marathon we're running. We need to profile everyone on the TruForce board of directors. With stuff like this, murder-for-hire, there's always a criminal conspiracy hidden away. We need to know everyone involved — who knew what — and when they knew it." He studied Finch for a moment as if he were trying to assess his stamina. "So prepare yourself. You never know where this

154

could lead."

※

After Wally opened the door and stepped into the rain, Finch made his way to the washroom. The news about Jojo had hit him hard, and he decided to call Biscombe to see what he'd learned from the police. After he relieved himself, he went to the cashier and asked if he could use the phone.

"The *phone?*" The cashier's tone sounded a note of surprise. "You're in luck, my friend. There's two pay phones on the wall next to the men's room."

He pointed to the corridor that Finch had traversed on his way to the toilets. In his preoccupation with Jojo, he'd missed them.

"And somehow that makes me lucky?" Finch felt as if he'd missed the punchline to a joke.

"Yeah. AT&T is yanking them out tomorrow. Nobody uses them anymore. In fact, you might win the prize for making the last call."

Finch smiled at that. The prize. His hand swept through his pockets for loose change. He pulled out two dimes. "Can you break a one for me and give me four quarters?" He drew a dollar bill from his wallet and pointed it at the payphone.

"See what I mean? They're way more trouble than they're worth." The cashier seemed to be in a good mood. Why not? The bar was hopping and everyone working the floor was raking in close to twenty percent in tips. He laughed and swapped the paper for coins.

Finch inserted a quarter into the phone and punched in Biscombe's number. One of the few he'd memorized. His friend answered on the third ring.

"Hey, Bisk. Just checking in." He could hear the sound of a TV in the background. "Where are you?"

"Home. Having a beer. Just watching the game highlights. Looks like the Boston Red Sox are headed to the World Series."

"Wow. That's something. Maybe they'll finally break The Curse of the Bambino."

"No, they broke that in oh-four against the Cards. You haven't been paying close enough attention." The background noise of the TV fell off. Biscombe must have turned the volume down. "Maybe you were somewhere else back then."

"I guess." Finch let this pass. Biscombe knew Will was posted to Abu Ghraib in 2004. Besides, the sports talk was nothing more than a diversion. He could tell by the sound of his voice that Biscombe was in a funk. They both loved baseball, but Will knew he couldn't waste any time on it. Not tonight.

"So listen. You went down to the cop shop today, right?"

"That I did."

"And you talked to Staimer again?"

A pause.

"Bisk, don't get me to drag this out of you word by word. One of the reporters at the *Post* says Jojo was found in a park. What happened man?"

He sighed. "It's bleak."

"I know. It's like the weather. But hell, you still have to go outside." A weak analogy, but Will didn't bother to elaborate. "Tell me what you know."

"All right. The forensics aren't wrapped up yet, but it sounds like he cut her throat."

It confirmed Wally's silent gesture. His fingers cutting across the thick flesh of his neck. "And where exactly did they find her?"

"Two tourists from Paris found her under some shrubs at El Polin Spring in the Presidio. It's a little hilltop in the park. You drive up, loop through the turn-around. Done deal. All under five minutes. You seen it? Five or six blocks from her foster home."

Finch hadn't heard of El Polin Spring, but he knew the Presidio. Once an old military post — now a national park with over fifteen hundred acres — it stretched from the Golden Gate Bridge to Presidio Heights. Hundreds of nooks and crannies dotted the forest trails where a body could be dropped off and made to disappear for a few days.

"Did he say if she'd been killed in the park or somewhere else?"

"They don't know yet."

"What else?"

"Nothing else."

Finch stared through the length of the lounge. Novela was still buzzing, the Thursday night party mood amping up with every fresh drink. "All right. Thanks, Bisk."

"Now I've got a question for you, my friend."

"For me? Shoot."

"How many people were in the apartment on Monday night?"

"You mean when Esposito went through the window?"

"Right. Besides you, how many?"

"Four. Jojo, Esposito, Henman. And Madden, according to Jojo, but I didn't see him."

"So now there's just you and Madden left."

Will considered this a moment. "You think that I'm —"

"I don't know, but Madden's still out there. The cops have put out a BOLO, but until he's in custody…." His voice trailed off.

Be On the Look Out. Sometimes they worked, sometimes not. As he absorbed the implications, a dull feeling sank through Finch's chest. He never considered that he might be targeted. And there was Cecily. Could she be vulnerable, too?

After a moment Biscombe's voice came back through the line. "Do you understand what I'm saying?"

Finch nodded to himself. "Yeah. I hear you."

"Stay alert. This guy's a pro. And he plays for keeps."

CHAPTER FOURTEEN

FINCH INSERTED ANOTHER quarter in the payphone and dialed Cecily's office number. He glanced at his watch. Ten after six. Not much chance that she'd still be at her desk, but worth checking. After four rings, a programmed message cut in announcing the library administrative office hours and he hung up. Next, he called the phone in their apartment. He heard his voice come over the line and waited for the message to end.

"Hey Cecily, it's me. I'm on time for once, and I'll hop on a BART train in the next ten minutes. How 'bout we meet at Kiraku and I'll buy you that sushi dinner I've been promising. Say, seven o'clock, okay? Love you."

He hung up, pleased that he'd said something to get her out of the apartment without ringing any alarm bells. Biscombe's warning had sent a shiver through him. An element of paranoia. He now felt an urgency about protecting Cecily. Then he considered the state of his anxiety and concluded that he'd become somewhat irrational. Which is what fear always did.

He steered his way through the after-work crowd at Novela, stepped along Jessie Street to Second, turned right onto Market and down into the Montgomery Street station. When he'd started the Master of Journalism program at Berkeley, the Bay Area Rapid Transit became his go-to form of transportation. He didn't own a car, and he'd sold his Honda Nighthawk motorcycle before he'd shipped off to Afghanistan and then Iraq. The BART lines had become the arteries and veins of his transit through the city. Part of his own body.

Although the rush hour was winding down, all the seats in his car were occupied. He clung to a handrail and studied the people surrounding him. As the train lurched forward, he braced himself against a closed door. Two tall, lean teenagers, their arms burdened with bags of groceries, stumbled next to him. The crush of the human zoo.

As he scanned the faces surrounding him, he recalled Felix Madden's photograph. Why had Blomquist faxed Madden's picture to Seamus Henman? It remained one of the unsolved problems in the story. Finch put together a likely scenario. Henman had asked Blomquist for some muscle to back up the blackmail sting against Gio Esposito. Just in case. Blomquist recommended his man, Madden. He'd show up at the apartment after Jojo was cuffed to the bed.

How do I recognize him? Seamus would have asked.

Simple. I'll fax his picture to you.

Finch imagined Blomquist saying these exact words. Dressed in his pinstripe suit sitting in his home office on Nob Hill. No idea that the fax would provide a direct link from Henman back to him. That was the sort of sloppiness that emerged from a series of mounting successes. An ego that ignored the laws of gravity. A condition that Finch's father had called "too smart by half."

At the far end of the car stood a man with a fixed expression on his face, a glare that showed a measure of determination. Could it be Madden? No. His eyebrows lay flat under his forehead, and his face was oval, not square. He continued to stare past Finch as if he saw someone coming toward him. Finch turned, but no one was moving. Everyone stood locked in place as the car pulled into Embarcadero station. The doors slid open and discharged hundreds of passengers onto the concourse. A new rank of strangers immediately replaced them. The doors shunted together and the familiar motion began again as the train burrowed down and under San Francisco Bay and onward toward Oakland and Berkeley.

From the Downtown Berkeley station, he walked along the south side of the university campus on Bancroft Way, turned right on Telegraph Avenue and down five or six blocks to Blake Street. Just past the corner stood Kiraku, a tiny — but almost perfect — Japanese tapas restaurant. He stepped under the sidewalk awning and through the door. The restaurant hummed with laughter and gossip from the college crowd that had turned Kiraku into one of the centers of off-campus life. He scanned the open room and made his way over to the bar where Yuki stood next to the till.

"Hi, Will. Haven't seen you in a week or two."

She embraced him and he kissed her cheek.

"I know. Been way too busy. Listen, have you seen Cecily?" He checked his watch. Five past seven. "I was supposed to meet her here around seven."

"No." A blank look crossed her face — then a flashing smile as she waved a new waiter towards her. "Goro, six bottles of Asahi to table six, okay?

"Sorry, Will. You can sit at the bar and wait for her if you want. Should be a table free in about ten minutes, okay?"

He considered this and decided to wait. He pointed to the far end of the bar. "Can I use the phone?"

"Local call?"

He nodded.

"Of course!" She offered another flash of her brilliant smile and turned to talk to Goro again.

"Thanks." He settled on a stool and pulled the telephone toward him. It was a punch-button style phone, and as he tapped in his home number, he thought about getting a new cellphone. He'd need one when he started full-time shifts at the *Post*. Maybe the paper offered a discount plan for reporters. He waited for four rings and their answering machine cut in. He briefly debated whether to leave another message.

"Cecily? Me again. I'm at Kiraku. Yuki's got a table for us. Should be free by the time you get here. Say, seven-twenty. Okay. See you soon."

He recognized the pleading sound in his voice. As if by merely saying these words aloud, Cecily would magically appear.

With a cellphone pressed to her ear, Yuki slipped behind the bar and set a white porcelain teacup in front of him, waved at him with her free hand, then eased back toward the cash register talking in Japanese as she moved back and forth.

He lifted the cup to his lips and inhaled the aroma. Jasmine. He took a sip and turned in his seat so that he faced the front door. Then he rechecked his watch and decided he would hold up until seven-thirty. As he waited, the events of the past few days swept through him. Everything had changed since he'd left Cafe Zoetrope last Monday night. It seemed like a year ago that he'd been talking about the final game of the baseball season with Biscombe, Jerry, and Phil. Their beer league. The semi-final game was scheduled for Sunday afternoon. Everyone was pumped.

He'd enjoyed the distraction and fun that the game offered. The post-game drinking. The laughs. The machismo he acquired from hitting a three-run homer in the previous game. But after their meal, during his stroll from the cafe to the Montgomery Street BART station, Gio Esposito had fallen from the sky and hit the sidewalk. That marked the instant his life crossed a particular junction of time and space. Now he wondered what the hell had become of his fiancée. It all tied together. A single, linear path from one moment to the next. From a moment of dread (Esposito's death) to this moment of anxiety (Cecily's absence). Esposito and Cecily had never met, never heard of one another. But now here they were, chained to Finch's karmic wheel.

Seven-thirty came and went with no sign of Cecily. Will finished his tea, left a dollar bill on the bar and made his way through the crowded doorway. He glanced left, then turned right along Telegraph Avenue toward his home.

※

As Finch marched up Dwight Way, he noticed that the sky was clear. For the first time in days, the steady rainfall had come to a halt. An on-shore breeze was blowing the three-day storm east over the Berkeley Hills toward the Central Valley and up into the Sierra Nevada Mountains. Autumn had finally arrived and the evening air felt crisp and fresh on his skin.

He crossed to the south side of the street. Given his anxious mood, he thought it better to avoid the drifters who passed through Peoples Park. In the sixties, the block-long green space had been taken over by hippies. They'd fought, and won, a political battle to claim the park as a public space. The hippies were long gone now, and the park had become a camp for what Finch called the helpless homeless. Usually, he maintained an abiding sympathy for them, and when he had a few spare coins, he would pass them on to those who held out an empty hat or tin can. But not tonight. The fact that Felix Madden remained on the loose did not reassure him.

As he passed the park, he could make out a lone man in the shadows, a figure standing apart from the cluster of tents on the far side of the sidewalk. He tried to think past his paranoia. Put it away and confront his fears. He knew it was the only way to stay sane.

He waited for a string of cars to drive past him, then crossed the road and stopped to face the stranger. Finch stood about ten feet away from him. The man appeared to be over six feet — Will's height, maybe an inch shorter. Because the lamplight cast his shadow in front of him, Finch couldn't make out any facial features. His thick chest, partially covered by a red-checked lumber jacket reminded Finch of a heavy-weight boxer. Slow, lumbering — but powerful.

Finch took a step forward onto the worn grass and said, "Hey friend, how're you doin'?"

The man shifted his weight to his right leg. A gust of wind

flapped the front of his jacket against his belly.

"Nice to get a break from this rain, huh?"

No reply.

Finch considered the options. He could move on or press harder. He decided to press. "Are you Felix Madden?"

The man began to button his jacket from the bottom up.

"I said, are you Felix Madden?"

Another button. And another.

"Never heard of him," the stranger whispered in a whiskey voice.

"No?" Finch glanced away. At that moment he felt absurd. Here he stood on a park sidewalk interrogating a complete stranger. A man he imagined might be a person he'd never met — but someone he'd come to dread. He pulled his jacket collar against his neck and wondered how he could clear this madness from his mind. He fished another dollar bill from his wallet and handed it to the drifter.

"All right, take this pal." Finch waved a hand in the air to suggest he couldn't quite believe his own mistake. "Sorry for the confusion."

A hint of surprise crossed the man's face. As he shoved the bill into his pant pocket, his expression turned to one of gratitude. "You keep dry now."

"You, too."

"And thank you."

Finch crossed Dwight again, and when he reached Benvenue Avenue, he traversed to the near corner. He stepped into the lobby of his apartment building, the Riviera Apartments. At one time the name of the building made him smile. Berkeley was closer to Tokyo than the French Riviera. On the day he'd signed the apartment lease he'd made a joke about it with the landlord.

A blast of wind kicked at the door. The rattling made him want to check the stairwells and corridors. He walked past the elevator bay and pushed open the door to the staircase. As he climbed up to the second floor, he could hear a loose downspout clattering against the exterior siding. He paced along the length of the hallway, up the far staircase to the third floor, then up the last flight of stairs to the fourth.

Will and Cecily rented a corner apartment on the top floor overlooking the parking lot. Not much of a view, but it was quiet, and they liked the privacy. As Finch approached his door, he checked over his shoulder. Nothing. His mood brightened a little as he talked himself into dismissing his fears. He unlocked the door and moved inside.

"Cecily?"

Silence.

He clicked on the hall light and sniffed the air. In the kitchen, the scent of stale coffee hung in the air. In the morning he'd been in such a rush to get to the office that he'd left his coffee mug next to the kettle without taking a second sip.

"Cecily, you here?"

He peered into the living room. An open, all-in-one space, it served as kitchen, dining and living room. At the far end, sliding glass doors opened onto a narrow deck that overlooked the neighborhood.

Next to the lounger, he spotted the red light blinking on the Panasonic answering machine. He pressed the PLAY button and heard his two messages to her. The third was from her to him.

"Hey Will. Guess what? I left my keys at the office. You got my note, I hope. So this is just a reminder that I'm at Gillian's for book club tonight. Anyhow, I should be back around eleven. Unlock the main door when I buzz, okay? Love you."

Her note?

He sauntered over to the table next to the balcony where they ate their meals. At the place where he usually sat lay a slip of paper torn from a memo pad she kept in her purse. The note read: "I'm off to book club at Gillian's tonight. Back around 11. xx oo."

He exhaled a long sigh of relief. He reread the note a second time and wondered about his mental state. Again, in his morning rush, he'd missed this. And he'd completely forgotten about the book club, a group of nine women who meet each month. This time around they were going to discuss Earl Derr Biggers's crime novels from the 1920s and 30s. The *Charlie Chan* series, of all things. Obviously, his fears and anxiety had been stirred by too little sleep and not enough food. No wonder he'd been paranoid.

He moved to the refrigerator, scanned the contents and decided to prepare a ham, pickle and cheese sandwich on rye bread. He ate at the table next to the balcony doors and gazed through the window. The wind tugged at the shrubs along the side of the fence. The lamppost cast a yellow glow onto the damp driveway. No sign of Cecily. No sign of Madden.

He moved to the futon sofa and propped his legs on the

coffee table that he'd bought last week at a garage sale on Derby Street. At the same sale, Cecily had picked up a crystal cake platter, the old-fashioned kind that stood on a single, three-inch glass stem. She had a "nesting instinct" she said. She planned to bake cookies and cakes and display them on the platter so that when the baby came, visitors could enjoy a small treat. There'd be coffee, tea, wine, cheese. And the new baby, of course.

He reread Cecily's note and chided himself for missing it during his morning rush. He knew he'd overextended himself and the pressure had made him sloppy. His errors pointed to the same lesson that he'd learned one too many times in Iraq: Waste yourself, waste your life.

He brushed his teeth, stripped off his clothes and climbed into bed. Counting backward from his next seven AM shift at the *Post*, he decided to set the alarm for five-thirty. As he drifted off, he commanded himself to remain alert for Cecily. She'd buzz him from the lobby, and he'd let her in, then he could crash. If things went his way, maybe he could get in six hours of rest.

※

He'd fallen far into the abyss, and now he drifted in a dead, unbroken sleep. On the third ring, the sound of the door buzzer shot him bolt upright. His eyes blinked open, and he clicked on the bedside lamp.

As he swung his legs onto the floor, he remembered. Cecily. He glanced at the clock: 11:21. He raked his fingers through his hair and padded across the hall carpet wondering if he should throw on a bathrobe. If she wanted to, they could sit up and talk. On the other hand, he felt so tired that he knew he'd make miserable company. Forget it, he whispered to himself.

He buzzed down to her.

"It's me," she called through the intercom. Her voice sounded bright, but weary from her long day.

"Okay," he said. "I'm in bed. It's open."

He unlocked the door and swiveled the swing bar lock between the doorframe and the entrance to ensure it remained open until she arrived. Then he returned to the bedroom and slipped under the covers. In his mind, he could see himself crawling back into the emptiness of sleep. It had been such a good, dreamless sleep. After a few seconds, he thought he'd found the edge of it, the lip where he could roll over and fall in. Then he heard her cry out.

"Will! *No. Stop it! Will!*"

Her voice dashed a chill through his veins. In an instant, he knew what had happened. In three steps he leaped through the bedroom into the hallway. Cecily's head was pressed against the wall. Her face was mottled with red splotches, her eyes wide with terror.

"I'm sorry," she whispered.

Finch studied the man beside her — glowering back at him. The thick ridge of eyebrows, the square face, the dimple punctuating his chin. Shaggy, jet black hair. Lips so thin they seemed invisible. In his left hand Felix Madden held a narrow open blade with a slight curve at the tip. An eight-inch filleting knife.

"Do as I tell ya or I slit her ear to ear," he whispered.

"No problem." Finch held up two hands in a defensive gesture.

"I see you forgot to dress for the 'casion." Felix Madden's voice had a hoarse, raw tone. With his right hand still pinning Cecily's head to the wall, he kicked the door behind him with a foot. It swung shut, and the deadbolt clicked. Then he pushed Cecily ahead of him into the living room. Will stepped forward so that he stood between them.

"So you're the reporter." Madden's mouth curled into a downward sloping smile. He waved the knife at Finch's belly with a casual swing of his arm.

Finch covered his genitals with his hands. "Let me get dressed."

"No. This is better. I'm sure your wife likes it, too. You prancing around all buck naked like that. Maybe if things went right, she'd have one in the oven, huh?" His face widened, and he broke into a laugh. The sick, cynical sneer matched his voice. "You ever had one, honey?"

Cecily stared at him, unable to speak.

"I said, *you ever had one?*"

"What?"

"A baby."

"No," she whispered and glanced at Will, terror haunting her face.

Finch drew a long breath. He knew what was coming. Knew he had to prepare.

"Well, they say first baby's the hardest. After that" — he made a long slicing motion with the knife — "they're supposed to jus' slide out."

170

Cecily whimpered and drew her hands over her mouth.

"Felix, your business is with me." Finch narrowed his eyes. Somehow he had to establish some leverage. He moved his hands from his crotch and set them on his hips. A gesture to show Madden that he wasn't afraid. "Let her go. Then we can settle up."

"Settle up?" Another laugh. "Nope. She stays." Madden's eyes wandered over Finch's body. He shook his head with a kind of false gaiety. "Hey now, you been keepin' yourself in good shape. Yeah, real buff."

Finch tried to imagine what he could seize for a weapon. The dinner knife he'd used to cut his sandwich in two. That was on the table near the balcony. Cecily's glass serving platter on the coffee table. His baseball bat stowed under the futon.

"Let's everyone sit down. Have a little chin-wag. You know, sociable." He swung the knife in a wide arc. "Before the main entertainment begins."

"Cecily, sit beside me." Finch moved toward the futon sofa. He sat on the right, just above the baseball bat. He kept it there along with his catcher's mitt and a few baseballs. Cecily sat beside him. She covered her eyes with a hand. The coffee table stood between them and the lounge chair where Madden settled into place. Finch noticed a dark bloodstain on the knife blade.

"How'd you find me?"

Madden pointed the knife to the telephone next to his chair. "You get a landline, you get a free listing in AT&T's phonebook."

"And then?" Finch wanted to keep him talking. Make time so that he could find a vulnerability of some kind. A weakness that he could exploit.

"Then I just followed your sweet piece through the door when you buzzed her in."

Cecily glanced at Finch and shook her head as if she couldn't bring herself to acknowledge what she'd done.

"Not your fault," he said.

"Maybe not," Madden said, "but let's talk about *whose* fault it is that young girl died. Huh?"

As he spoke Madden's eyes widened. The pupils appeared to be fully dilated. Finch wondered if he was high on methamphetamines. Or maybe crack cocaine. When the time came to fight him, he'd be barbaric. Finch knew he'd have to move fast. The battle would last three, maybe four strokes, and be done.

"You mean Jojo? The one you cuffed to the bed."

"Me? That was Henman. He was all about the chickies."

"She said she knew you."

"Oh yeah, we had our time or two." He laughed again. "Or three or four. Young wildcat she was."

Finch shrugged and glanced away. "Tell me something, Felix. How did you and Julian Blomquist hook up?"

"You wanna know? Really?" His bright mood continued. But it was all a sham. Finch doubted Madden was capable of expressing an honest emotion.

"Yeah. I do."

"We're cousins. On my mama's side."

"Cousins?"

"Grew up on opposite sides of the track. But as they say, blood runs thicker than water." He raised his free hand as if he were pledging an oath. "Ha. I can testify to that."

Finch tried to conceal his disbelief. He wondered how much Madden would reveal about Seamus Henman. "Speaking of Henman, how did that work?"

"What'd'ya mean *work?*"

"You know. The five knives thing. Where'd you get that?"

"You wondering about that, huh?" Madden crooked his head to one side to emphasize just how clever he'd been. "Let me put it this way, a lot of stories run through Ironwood."

Ironwood State Prison. Cecily had found it in her research of the telephone numbers. "You spent a little time there I understand."

"More than a little." He spat on the floor.

"So?"

"So men have ears. Men have lips. In a place where there's nothin' more to trade than stories, you hear things."

"Like the five knives murders in Wichita and Reno."

When Madden didn't respond, Finch pressed him. "And you thought you'd try it on Henman."

"Got your attention, didn't it?"

His face revealed a bland indifference. Finch wondered how much longer he could stall. Then it occurred to him. He'd crossed paths with Madden before. In the corridor outside the Versatile Property Group office where Gio Esposito had cooked up his mortgage packages.

"You know, I've seen you before."

"Don't think so." Madden rubbed his left hand over his right shoulder. "I remember faces. Not yours."

"That's because you had your mind on other things."

"What other things?" He seemed curious now.

"Tuesday afternoon. Just outside Esposito's office. Think back."

Madden's eyes narrowed as he tried to summon the memory. "Yeah?"

"I was just going in the door and you were coming out."

"Maybe." He waved a hand. "Who gives a shit?"

Finch paused. "You'd just gone into Esposito's office. You found his laptop, didn't you?"

He blinked and turned away as if to deny this petty theft.

"And you took it to Blomquist. It was the one thing he *had* to get, wasn't it?"

"This is getting tired." He drew a deep breath and switched the knife to his free hand.

Finch knew that he'd finally found some leverage and had to keep the pressure on. He decided to turn the conversation back to Jojo.

"So why'd you kill her, Madden?"

"Jojo?" He grimaced as if he regretted it. "After I saw her name in your paper. Then she just had to go. Specially with my face on the cover." His voice hinted at some surprise. Perhaps he never expected to see his mug shot — the same image Julian Blomquist had faxed to Seamus Henman — on the front page of the *Post.* He turned away as if he needed to sort out the details. "Same reason you got to go, my friend. Jojo said you were up in the apartment with her. Like my cousin used to say, 'witnesses never prosper.' Sad but true."

"That doesn't mean shit, and you know it. You didn't have to kill her. You did it for pleasure."

Madden's leathery face tightened, and the muscles around

his jaw clenched. "You know Finch, you get boring real fast."

"Boring?" Finch's laugh sounded hollow. A mockery. "The cops are all over this. You've got one, two days at the most before they bring you down."

Madden shifted the knife to his right hand and rubbed his right shoulder. A glint of pain flashed through his face. After massaging the shoulder, he transferred the blade back to his left hand.

Was he left-handed or did he favor that side? Then Finch knew. An injury to his right shoulder. Maybe it was slight, perhaps little more than a torn rotator cuff — but it was an opening.

"Enough talk." Madden snorted, and his nostrils flared. "Sweetheart, I want you to come over here now."

"No." Finch put his hand on her forearm. "She doesn't move. It's time for you to leave, Felix. Before it's too late."

"*Too late?* Fuck you, asshole."

Madden stood up and took a step to the left to move around the coffee table. On his second step, Finch stood to face him. As he rose up, he grabbed the crystal platter by the stem and thrust it forward like a shield.

Madden swung the blade in a broad slash aimed at Finch's belly. The steel chinked against the glass and broke off a long splinter that exposed a sharp edge. He lunged again at Finch and cut a three-inch laceration along his left forearm. At the same time, Finch made a second thrust with the platter and caught Madden under the chin and just above his larynx. The blow shattered the glass into a dozen pieces that fell to the floor.

"Fuck!" Madden gasped and stepped to his left. He pressed his free hand to his throat and examined the smeared blood in his palm.

Finch ignored his wound, reached under the sofa and drew the baseball bat into his hands. He kicked the coffee table toward Madden. It brushed against Madden's left shin as it thudded to the floor. Finch now had room to move. He held the barrel of the bat in front of him with the knob end at his waist. He could see the cut on his arm was bleeding, but Madden's injury seemed more dangerous.

"Your throat's cut bad, Madden. Time to call this off."

Madden's face lit up with fury. "Fuck you!"

He shifted the filleting knife to his left hand — an awkward move that assured Finch that his opponent was right-handed and forced by an injury to fight with his weaker hand. He began slashing the knife through the air from side to side.

With his eyes steadily focused on the knife, Finch parried with the bat. He pumped the wood spindle in narrow bunts that kept Madden at bay. Madden's face knotted in frustration. After a moment a blind rage overtook him, and he lunged forward. With a firm slap, Finch smacked the knuckles of Madden's hand and the knife flew against the near wall and clattered against the floor. Finch then speared the bat into Madden's chest just above his solar plexus. Madden gasped for breath and took a step backward. Then another back-step, and another, struggling for breath as he moved. Finch moved forward, stride for stride, keeping Madden in his range, waiting for the right moment. When he saw it — Madden clutching at his throat with his left hand — Finch raised the bat over his head and swung it down into Madden's right shoulder. Will heard the taut *pop* as the collarbone snapped and Madden collapsed on the floor. As he lay on the carpet, he began to inhale short sips of air. His eyes fluttered with pain. A dull moan erupted from his mouth.

Finch stood above him and threatened him with the bat. "You want any more?" His voice brimmed with outrage and anger. He tried to lock it down, but the adrenaline surged through him.

"I said, you want any more?!"

"Will ... stop."

Cecily's voice washed over him. A whisper, a wish — a warm breeze from another world.

With his eyes fixed on Madden, he drew two deep breaths. The fight was over, but he knew he couldn't let Madden up. Never again. He drove the heel of his right foot into Madden's ribcage, a bruising kick to serve as a warning.

"Cecily, call 9-1-1. Then get me something for this cut," he gasped. He coughed to clear his throat. "And toss me my pants, too."

The blood seeped steadily along his arm to his wrist and into his hands where he gripped the baseball bat in his fists. His flesh had been pared away on his forearm, exposing the bands of extensor muscles. None of his arteries appeared to be severed, but the wound was deep, and now the pain began to sharpen and intensify.

From somewhere in the back of his mind he asked himself, *Do I have your attention?* Yes, he answered. This is real. This is here and now. And it's over.

Cecily made the call to the police. As she moved to the bathroom to find a compress and bandages, Finch peered into Madden's black, dilated eyes.

"You try to get up, and I'll take your fucking head off." He could still feel the adrenaline pumping through him. "Do you hear me?"

With one hand cradling his shoulder, Madden blinked and twisted away.

"I said, do you *hear* me?" He swung the bat above Madden's head, and a dash of blood from his arm flecked along Madden's right cheek.

"Yeah," he whispered. "I hear you."

CHAPTER FIFTEEN

FINCH NEEDED SEVEN subcutaneous stitches to repair the damage to the muscles in his forearm. He also required a tetanus shot, a "necessary precaution," the doctor said after the forensic team determined that Madden's filleting knife was the same blade he'd used to kill Jojo.

Then came the question of HIV infection. Jojo's autopsy revealed that she'd been HIV-positive. The news sent Finch into a funk. If Madden hadn't murdered her, her health would be hijacked by a course of antiretroviral drugs. And if her luck didn't hold, she'd have to fight a day-to-day battle against AIDS. One more hurdle to jump. Perhaps one too many. Fortunately, she never knew her condition.

Although transmission of infected blood from the steel blade was improbable, the possibility threw a scare into Cecily. So before they left the hospital, Will provided a blood sample for analysis and was promised a result by Monday afternoon.

Cecily rolled her eyes. She'd imagined that a simple in-house screen would provide an immediate result. "So now we have to wait all weekend?" she asked.

"Don't worry, Cecily," he told her. "It's very unlikely." But he didn't let on that he was worried, too.

After his discharge from the hospital, they endured an hour-long questioning from the Berkeley PD, then made their way home. They spent another hour arm-in-arm comforting one another in bed. Soon after, they decided to push themselves to go back to work. "Let's get some sleep, then just carry on," Will said. Cecily didn't need any convincing. By five o'clock they both slipped into a heavy, unbroken sleep.

The next morning, as Cecily left the apartment and made her way over to her office at Berkeley, Finch ate some toast and washed down a Tylenol Three tablet with some coffee. He sat alone at the breakfast table to consider his next move. He knew he had to get back to the *Post* to file a report about the attack and Felix Madden's arrest. But then he considered a more pressing issue. Something he needed to know before he could push the story forward.

※

Will stepped into the dull light of the 500 Club and spied J.R. sitting near the far wall at his favorite table. Although Finch's world had been tossed upside down and sideways, it appeared that nothing much had altered the life of Jeremy Rickets since they'd met here yesterday. He still wore the same clothes. Still nursed a glass of Miller. The demeanor on JR's face hadn't changed much either. The puffy cheeks, the heavy eyelids.

As he stepped toward the table, Finch didn't bother to put on a smile.

"You not drinking?" J.R. asked, alluding to the fact that Will hadn't stopped at the bar to order a beer. "Or is one o'clock too early for you?"

"I have to stay sharp," Will said and sat with his back facing the room. A gesture to show J.R. that he wasn't troubled by paranoia. He set his courier bag on the floor and tried to relax.

"I'm surprised you took my call," Finch said. "Don't get me wrong — I'm glad you did. Just surprised is all."

"Me too. I don't know what it is. Maybe not being able to let go is the worst part of this thing."

This thing. Finch knew that he meant the PTSD. Mental illness with claws so long it latched onto the inside of your skull and dug in. From there it spawned and bred unending nightmares and ghosts. Finch decided not to reply. The worst thing he could do was open the door to JR's on-going horror.

A moment later J.R. continued. "So you say you've got something to share." He lifted his eyebrows with a skeptical gaze, took a drink from his glass and then added, "That's a very white word, by the way. *Share.*"

Finch smiled. "The other day you said I never give up anything. Today I'm just an average white guy. You can't have it both ways, J.R."

"Fuck you." His mouth looked ready to bite.

Finch held up both hands, his palms open. "Okay, my bad." His expression shifted to reveal a kind of shame. "Listen. Yesterday I was an asshole, and I know it." His gaze was steady. Sincere. "I apologize. You were a good man back in Iraq and I counted on you more than a few times."

J.R. nodded once, a slight gesture, and Will pressed on.

"I'm going to tell you some stuff that the FBI has kept under the lid. And stuff I know about this story I'm working on. That's it. After that, you don't need to say a word. You can walk out of here and pretend we never met. But if you do say anything and I use it in my reporting, I will protect you as a confidential source. No one will know about you. The only thing I ask is that you never repeat what I'm about to tell you."

J.R. took another sip of his beer and set the glass down. He passed a hand over his eyes and nodded again.

"The five knives killings that the FBI is tracking showed up in Wichita last April. Then in Reno in July. Then I found the same thing this week over in the Mission."

"You found it?"

"Yeah. I think it's related to a guy pushed from a window and killed in Chinatown on Monday. But it depends on whether his killer was a copycat. Or not."

J.R. blinked, a long pause with his eyes closed. Perhaps it was an attempt to shield himself from all the misery he'd seen. His eyes opened again. "Well, the big storms never blow in from one direction."

"No, I guess not."

"Believe me, they don't." J.R. seemed sure of it.

"So here's the thing, J.R. My guy died with his hands and his feet attached. And his balls on." Finch glanced away, then turned his attention back to J.R. "But in Wichita and Reno the hands and feet were severed. And both men castrated."

They considered this in silence for a moment. Then J.R. asked, "Peckers, too?"

"Yeah. That, too."

J.R. pinched his lips together and rolled his tongue over his teeth. The skin above and below his lips stretched tight, and it seemed as if he was preparing to spit out a wad of sputum that had crawled up his throat.

"And you want to know … what, exactly?"

"Like I said before. That's up to you."

"Bullshit." J.R. took another sip of beer and seemed to mull over everything he'd heard. He leaned forward and spoke in a voice so low that he was almost inaudible. "All right. The guy in Iraq? He cut them all. At least four of them. Hands, feet, peckers and balls. From what you say, then it's the same psycho in Kansas and Nevada. Your guy — leaves their parts on? *He's* the copycat."

Finch held himself from punching a fist in the air. He had it. A second source confirming that Madden was the copycat. The puzzle pieces now clicked together in a new way. He could almost hear them snap into place.

"But you didn't get it from me," J.R. added. "None of it. I'll deny it to the cops, and I'll never appear in court."

"You won't have to."

"No?"

"On my word, man. You're a protected source." Finch held his eyes. "Think back. I never lied to you. And I never broke my word to you."

"All right," J.R. rolled his lips in and out over his teeth as he considered another issue. "You know something?"

"What?"

"I figured it out after he left the sandbox. In oh-five. Too late to do anything about it."

"Figured what out?"

"The guy. Vincent Sessions. He was the perp."

"Vincent Sessions." Will repeated the words, but couldn't recall the name. "And there were no more killings after he moved on?"

"None. He disappeared, and that was the end of the game."

"You never told your CO?"

"No. He got reposted the week before I figured it out."

Finch considered this. Failure to report his findings was a serious breach of protocol. It could still put J.R. in legal jeopardy.

"Then what happened?"

"The new CO came in a month later. A certified moron. Everything went backwards. Everything." J.R. shook his head with exhaustion. "And that's when ... I just ran out of juice." He tried to smile. "When there was no more black on a bruise."

Finch didn't know how to respond. He waited to see if J.R. would say anything more.

"And the failure to report what I found out?" J.R. drew a long breath. "I know. Now the crime's on me. I own it. But you didn't hear that from me neither. Okay?"

"No, I didn't." Finch pulled his bag onto his lap and stood up. "Thanks," he said.

J.R. studied him for a moment and said, "You go lightly, Finch."

They traded a fist bump, and Will made his way through the door and onto Guerrero Street. A steady breeze was up. It dragged a dozen autumn leaves through the air, along the sidewalk and down the street where they stuck against a sewer grill. Soon, Finch thought, the fall winds will sweep through the city and everyone will forget the long storm that began on the night when Gio Esposito flew through the air.

※

It was past three o'clock when Finch returned to the *Post*. As he approached the reception desk, Dixie Lindstrom caught his eye and told him to join the meeting underway in the board-room. "They're going to be glad to see you." She smiled. "And so am I."

"Yeah. Nice to be seen."

She raised her hand. "Can you give this to Wally?" She passed him a folded slip of paper. "He needs to see it right away."

"Sure thing," he replied and made his way past the rows of cubicles to a wall panel marked BOARDROOM.

He knocked on the door and entered the long, narrow space. In the middle stood a large rectangular table that covered at least half of the room's footprint. Everyone appeared to be studying a document projected onto the white screen on the far wall. Wally swung around to face him.

"Well, well. Here's the hero of the hour." His face broke into a wide grin. "If you haven't met him yet, everyone, this is Will Finch."

A round of applause rang through the room. Wally introduced him to Ross Sumner, the business reporter whom Wally had assigned to handle background research on TruForce Investments. Next to him sat Lou Levine, the legal advisor for Parson Media, the corporate body that owned the *Post* along with six other publishing properties.

Finch shook their hands, then passed Dixie's note to Wally and sat next to Olivia.

Wally opened the note and tapped his knuckles on the table. "Happy days, folks. It appears that Julian Blomquist was taken into custody just before noon today."

Another cheer went up.

"So we've got a one-day lead on everyone else, but you can bet every media unit in the country will be on this story within the hour. I want everyone here to focus on this story and nothing else. So that means we're cleared for take-off, right?" He paused and glanced at Lou Levine for confirmation.

"Yes." The lawyer nodded. "You can report everything except the details on the five knives murders in Reno and Wichita. You can say Henman was killed by multiple knife wounds, but offer no details. And no photos."

He turned to Finch.

"I understand you have photographs of Henman?"

Finch nodded. "I do."

"Fine. Hang onto them. But until the feds clear us, we can't print them."

"There's something new on this," Will said and then wondered how to continue. His priority — to protect J.R. as his source — would have to be guarded carefully. "I have a lead on the original five knives serial killer."

No one said a word. After a moment Wally's chin dipped to one side as he leaned toward Finch.

"The original?" Wally said.

"He confirms the theory that Madden is the copycat." Finch turned from Wally to Olivia and back. "I have a name of someone linked to similar killings in Iraq. A soldier who may be responsible for four knife murders before he was discharged."

A light buzz hummed through the room. Lou Levine held up a hand to silence everyone. "Don't say another word. If you have something — I mean *really* something — on this then we have to disclose it to the FBI. And I mean right now." He glowered at Wally to emphasize the pressing urgency.

Wally nodded to Levine. The lawyer stood up, slipped around the table and tapped Finch's shoulder. "Come with me," he murmured and led him through the door.

※

Lou Levine's office was at the back of the *Post* building on the third floor. The window behind his desk looked onto Minna Street. The adjacent wall held three framed parchment degrees from Stanford, Berkeley, and Harvard. Next to his desk stood two pairs of chrome-framed leather chairs. A glass coffee table separated the two groupings. The zen-like arrangement suggested that it was a space designed for calm, reasoned mediation — as opposed to brass-knuckled legal brawling reserved for the courts. Over a hundred hardcover reference books lined another wall, legal tomes that Finch assumed were rarely pulled from their shelves. He knew that most legal research churned through the internet from legal databases like Lexus Nexus. Nonetheless, the books provided an air of credibility and Will reckoned that Levine was a competent advocate when he represented the legal interests of the *Post* — and by extension, the *Post's* employees.

Twenty minutes after Levine called Agent Raymond Albescu at the regional FBI office, he knocked on Levine's office door. Beside him stood his partner, Dan Busby. Levine shook their hands and directed them to the two leather chairs under the triptych of framed degrees.

Will recalled his previous meeting with the two agents. Somehow they appeared more vulnerable now. Busby easily filled a 48-medium jacket. Built like a center guard, he appeared ready to plow into a line of six men. His round head stood stock-still on his porcine neck. Albescu, on the other hand, seemed like an ex-basketball player. He stood tall and lean and bore a long, weary face etched with vertical worry lines. Despite their athletic builds, both men were well past their prime. For a brief moment, Will wondered if they'd both been benched for a few seasons and only called into action when the FBI needed all hands to solve the serial murders.

"I understand," Busby said, "that you've come across some information relating to the case we're working on." As Busby opened a file and placed it on his knees, Albescu pulled a small cassette recorder from his briefcase and set it on the glass coffee table.

"We'll be recording this," Albescu said and clicked the record button.

Finch recalled Albescu's tender, almost delicate, voice and the contrast to his leathery face. Surely the man had been destined to work as a choirmaster. But somehow he'd been sidetracked to a life spent chasing down the devil. Then again, Will thought, maybe the two careers weren't so different after all.

"Fine with us. Let's dig in," Levine said and waved a hand to dispense the formalities. "First, I want you to know that when Will brought this information to our attention, I called you within ten minutes."

"Duly noted," Busby said and turned to Will. "So what do you have?"

"A name."

Busby forced a smile to his lips. "Good. And what is it?

"Before I tell you, I need to be sure that we're talking about the same person. In this case, I'm *not* referring to Felix Madden, the man who stabbed Seamus Henman."

Again, Lou Levine held up a hand in a bid to provide clarification. "I don't know if you'd heard this yet, but Madden was brought into the Berkeley PD by Will last night."

Busby nodded, a bare acknowledgment of the battle in Finch's apartment.

"Understood," Albescu said. "So who *are* you talking about?"

Finch set his elbows on his knees and leaned forward. "Like I said, I want to know something about the man you're looking for."

"What?" Busby frowned and shook his head with a scowl of impatience. "Finch — it doesn't work that way. You tell us what you've got. Then we decide how to proceed."

Finch glanced at Levine. The lawyer returned his look with a gesture that said, don't play games.

"All right. This guy does the five knives cuts just the way Madden did it to Henman. Belly, ribs, heart, throat, ear." Will raised his hand and counted off his fingers, one for each laceration. "But here's the thing. Madden is a copycat killer. The original killer also severed the hands and feet of each victim."

Busby's eyes narrowed. "And?"

"And their testicles and penises."

189

D. F. Bailey

Busby studied Albescu — who nodded once. When Finch
saw the gesture of agreement between the two cops he knew he
was close.

Busby dropped his hands into his lap. "So now we'd like
that name, Finch."

"I'll tell you." He lifted his hands from his knees and sat
back in the chair. "But I want you to confirm that we're talking
about the same perp. And if he *is* the same killer, I want an
exclusive interview with you about this *new* case."

Busby's face began to flush. He drew a breath and leaned
toward Will. "Okay. No more fucking around. We already
guaranteed you an exclusive." Busby glanced at his watch.
"Three days ago. Now you can give us the name right now, or
we'll charge you for impeding an investigation and take you
down to our office for interrogation."

Busby's voice was hard, unwavering. And unnerving. Finch
felt his heart sink into his stomach. He'd tried to leverage what
he had and lost. He glanced at Lou Levine, a plea for support,
but all the lawyer could do was offer a grimace that said, I told
you: don't try to play them.

"So. You gonna shit, or do we drag you off the pot?" Busby
held out a hand as if the choice was obvious.

It reminded Finch of the offer he'd made to Jojo. Why had
she taken the hard way out? He shuddered when he realized
just how badly his day could go from here. "All right." He took
another moment to think. "The name is Vincent Sessions. He
was on active duty in Baghdad until about 2005. The killings
stopped when he moved on."

"Army? Marines? Who?" This from Albescu.

190

"Army."

"Which unit?"

"I don't know."

"How many times did he strike?" Busby's gaze generated an intense energy that seemed to stir the air.

"At least four. I doubt anyone knows for sure."

"Four? Where'd you get this from?" Albescu asked in his heavy whisper.

Finch considered how to protect J.R. Now he had to be careful. "I was stationed in Abu Ghraib at the time. There'd been rumors of someone stabbing the locals — the Hajjis — in Baghdad. Since I was with Military Intelligence, I was ordered to check it out. Nothing clicked at the time." He paused to consider what to say next. Better to shut up, he decided.

"That's not what we asked," Busby leaned forward. "Vincent Sessions. *Who gave you the name?*"

Will realized that he'd reached the point of no return. He'd either have to lie or turn J.R. over to the feds. Or shield his source under the first amendment provisions. "I can't tell you that," he said. "He's a protected source."

"You can't be serious!" Busby stood up and wheeled about. His fists rolled into two hammers as he tried to restrain his temper.

"Detectives." Lou Levine held up a hand. "We have every right to protect our sources, and you know it. Now I called you here to advise you that we have a name. We've given it to you. Vincent Sessions. Our obligations — moral and legal — are fulfilled."

"Fuck!" Busby lifted his chrome chair by the back and

drove the legs onto the carpet.

"Dan," Albescu whispered. "We got the name. Let's find Sessions. We can deal with the source later."

Busby drew a loud breath. Once again he narrowed his eyes as he studied Finch. He seemed to be calculating the sum of information that Finch had added to what he already knew. "All right," he said, "we'll take it from here."

Albescu leaned forward and clicked off the cassette recorder.

"Let us know if you need anything more," Levine said and stood up. He faked a generous smile. "And thanks for coming down."

Albescu lifted the cassette deck from the coffee table and slipped it into his briefcase. Busby took his file in his hand. As they gathered their belongings, Busby said, "If this plays out — this lead to Vincent Sessions — we'll want to talk to you again."

"Fine," Will said as he rose from his chair. "Any time," he added, knowing that he had to stay on their side if the case broke open and he finally got his exclusive interview.

After the two agents left the office, Lou closed the door and turned to Will. "You're treading a fine line, Will. They could easily have cuffed you and taken you in."

"I was just playing for some leverage," he replied. "Isn't that what Wally would do?"

Levine laughed. "Yeah, you're right." Then with a frown, he added, "Sadly."

※

When Lou and Will returned to the boardroom, the editorial

meeting appeared to be wrapping up. Wally glanced at the lawyer and Will as they made their way to their chairs.

"You settle everything with the FBI?" The question was addressed to Lou, and then he turned his attention to Finch.

"I think so," Lou said in a voice that left room for doubt. "Will had to claim first amendment protection."

"Really?"

"I had to," Finch said and shrugged.

"Good. No need to apologize." Wally seemed pleased with the answer. "Stories like these push us to use all the resources we have. If you know you're right, stick to your guns.

"Okay. What else do we have?" Wally continued and glanced at Sumner and Olivia.

"My contact in the medical examiner's office whispered something over coffee this morning." Olivia folded her hands on the table. "A forensic detail that could be important."

"Tick-tock," Wally said with an impatient frown. "Don't make us guess."

"Sorry." She nodded and continued. "So apparently a trace of organic tissue found under Jojo's fingernails matches Madden's DNA."

After a moment's pause, Wally asked, "And that means what, exactly?"

"She must have cut him," Finch said. He turned to Olivia. "Were there any scratch wounds found on Madden?"

"I don't know." She shrugged and lifted her hands in an empty gesture.

"Well, when he attacked me, Madden was already injured," Finch said. "On his right shoulder."

Wally turned to Olivia. "Can you check it out?"

"I can try."

"That means she got her digs in. Literally," Finch said. "Before he killed her. She didn't go down without a struggle." Then he realized that without Jojo's first cut at Madden he wouldn't have been able to exploit the injury. Very likely, in fighting for her own life, she'd saved Will and Cecily.

Wally nodded, a silent acknowledgment that although she'd defended herself against a monster twice her size, the outcome was inevitable. He turned to Finch. "All right, that leaves your story, Will. Last night when Madden came for you. Are you ready to tell it?"

He set his hands flat on the table. "I think so."

"Good. Set aside a half hour with Olivia after we break. She'll run the interview. I want it on the front page tomorrow morning. That's priority one."

Finch felt a hint of betrayal. Suddenly the tables had been turned on him. "You mean I don't get to write it?"

"Not this one. You're the story, not the reporter."

"But —" He paused when a thin blade of pain shot along the length of his injured forearm.

Wally held up a hand. "Don't worry. You'll get to write the first-person feature sometime down the road. Once we have all the facts. It'll be the capstone story, I guarantee it. But not yet." He lowered his hand and continued. "Okay, priority two is yours, Ross. Backgrounders on all the TruForce board members and directors. Where do we stand on that?"

"Almost done. It'll be on your desk before I leave tonight," Sumner said. He brushed a six-inch-long band of blond hair from his eyes and tucked it over his left ear.

Apart from a brief greeting when they shook hands, this was the first time Finch had heard Sumner speak up. Until now, he seemed like an unknown quantity. But if he could provide a three-sixty view of TruForce, it would add an essential dimension to the story.

"Good," Wally replied. "Okay, so from what I can see, that leaves two unanswered questions. One: If the feds confirm that Felix Madden is *not* the five knives serial killer, how the hell did he know about it — and then do a copy-cat killing?"

"From Ironwood Prison," Finch said.

"Ironwood?"

"That's what he told me. He heard the story inside. As if the five knives murders were common knowledge. He said, 'men have lips, men have ears.' "

A grimace of disgust crossed Olivia's face. "Obviously, a master of human observation."

"Why would he tell you that?" Sumner asked. "It's completely self-incriminating."

"I don't know." Finch shrugged again. Now that he recalled what Madden said before their fight, he realized much of Madden's personality and motivations would remain a mystery. "I think he was ramped up on methamphetamines. He was injured. He had nowhere to run. So —"

"And he's a sociopath," Lou Levine cut in. "Sometimes there's no making sense of what they do."

"All right," Wally's tone suggested he wanted to move on. "Olivia, make sure you cover all that in your interview with Will. That takes us to question two: our missing link. How did

Julian Blomquist hook up with Felix Madden?"

Finch suppressed a smile as he glanced around the room. "Again, I can tell you what Madden told me." He still found the answer hard to believe. "They're cousins."

Olivia turned to him. "Cousins?"

"Really?" Wally lowered his jaw and studied Finch over the rim of his glasses.

"It was one of the last things he said to me." Finch nodded. "I can't imagine why he'd lie about it."

"No? Maybe not," Wally said. "Are you ready to dig in on that?"

"What do you mean?"

"Try to contact Blomquist's family members. If they won't talk to you, then run a check through the state birth, marriage and death registries. Check California first. If you come up empty then search state by state, going west to east."

"Sure thing," he said, his voice flat, almost inaudible. He didn't have a clue how to steer his way through these databases. Or where to begin.

Olivia noticed his puzzled expression and glanced at Wally. "Jeremy Costain can help him with that," she said as she turned back to Finch. "Record searches are his front and backyard."

"Right. Get Costain to pinch hit on this thing. Tell him I said to give you two hours of his time. Then after you verify the link between Blomquist and Madden," Wally continued, "write a sidebar on it."

"Got it," Finch said.

"At some point, we should determine how far back they've been running a kill book. Is this a one-off, or what?" His voice dropped to a baritone murmur. "And Lord help us if it isn't."

No one responded. Everyone appeared to understand that Wally's appeal to the Lord indicated the meeting was about to end.

"All right, that's it, people. Unless you're on the weekend desk, have a good weekend. I want everyone to report back here by noon on Monday. And remember why we do this." Wally's voice was brighter now. "Without the facts — without *the truth* — we can kiss this country goodbye."

At that moment Finch felt as if he'd arrived. He was part of the team now and he knew the story couldn't move forward without him. Depending on where the various threads of the crimes led, the *Post* would need him to weave the whole story together for weeks — maybe months — to come.

CHAPTER SIXTEEN

WILL RETURNED TO his desk on Monday morning and dug into the research linking Felix Madden and Paul Julian Blomquist. But as the morning wore on, connecting Blomquist to Madden became problematic.

As Wally predicted, none of the Blomquist family members would answer any of Finch's questions. First, he called his wife, Suzanne, who abruptly hung up when Finch identified himself as a reporter at the *Post*. His younger brother, Roman Blomquist, the director of communications at TruForce Investments, threatened to sue the *Post* (and Finch personally) before he cursed and hung up.

But with the help of Jeremy Costain, Finch discovered that Julian Blomquist and Felix Madden were indeed cousins. Within an hour, Costain's savvy navigation of the Vital Records section of the California Department of Public Health revealed that in 1968, eight-year-old Donna Rasmussen — later to become Felix Madden's mother — had been placed in foster care following her own mother's death from heart failure. After the state declared that it was unable to locate the eight-year-old's father, Alfred and Polly Wilmott formally adopted the orphaned girl and gave her their surname. They brought Donna into their home in Sacramento, at which point Donna became a stepsister to Josie, the Wilmott's biological daughter. In 1981, Josie married Abner Blomquist, a local insurance salesman. Ten months later Donna married Waylon Madden, a telephone lineman from Fresno. The stepsisters bore their first sons within two months of one another. The baby boys were technically cousins — but only in the legal sense of the word. And while they may not have been born psychopaths, together they had become something worse.

At the noon editorial meeting Finch made his report to Wally showing the connections linking Blomquist and Madden. He acknowledged that Jeremy Costain had figured it out. Then Will thanked Olivia Simmons and Ross Sumner for their support and direction. When the meeting wrapped up at twelve-thirty, Will had no doubts that he was a part of the team. Although a lot of work remained to report the full story, everyone was smiling.

High from the effervescent mood, he bought a ham-and-cheese sandwich on rye at Grove Yerba Buena, returned to the office and then started to write a criminal profile of Felix Madden. Just after two o'clock, he received a call from the blood lab.

"This is Agatha Castellanos. I have your blood test results." The voice had a formal, bureaucratic tone. "I can give them to you over the phone if you like. If not, I can mail them to you. Or I can do both."

"Yes. Of course," he said. "Over the phone." He drew a breath.

"Good news, Mr. Finch," she said, a little more personably. "Your profile came in HIV-negative."

He exhaled a sigh of relief. "So that means I'm clear? No chance of getting AIDS?"

"As of today, no. You're clear. As I said, it's good news." Now the lab tech's voice sounded almost affectionate. He could tell she was pleased, too. Likely she had to make several calls a day that went the other way.

"What about false negatives?" Part of him couldn't quite believe it. "Do you ever get those?"

"Rarely. Almost never." A pause. "You're good to go. Anything else I can do to help you?"

"No. I guess not."

"Great. Enjoy your love life." She laughed and hung up.

He checked his watch. Cecily had probably finished her coffee break. He knew that she'd want to hear the news about his blood test. More important, he wanted to speak to her — to hear the sound of her voice. Within thirty seconds he'd connected with her from his desk phone.

"How's Momma doing today?" he asked.

"Momma's all right. For the first time, I'm definitely feeling pregnant." Her voice revealed a weariness. "It's kind of exhausting."

"I can imagine." In fact, he couldn't. Conception, pregnancy, and birth all remained mysterious to him. He understood them about as well as he understood the mystery behind quantum mechanics.

"So I just got the call from the blood lab." To tease her, he let the sentence hang.

"You did? *And?*" Her voice rose in anticipation. He knew she could tell the result was good.

"And I'm fine. HIV-negative."

"Fantastic. Great news."

"I know. It is."

A moment of silence slipped between them. Will wanted to let her move the conversation forward, let her decide if she wanted to talk about Madden's attack on them. She did.

"You still thinking about what happened?" she asked.

"Not so much now. It's over and done with."

After a pause, she said, "Yeah I can see that in you. I don't know how you do that."

"It's a kind of focus." He thought for a moment. "You think of something else, something better — like the baby — and concentrate on that."

"As simple as that?" She sounded dismissive. "They taught you this in the army?"

"No. Not the army." He felt like changing the focus right now. "How 'bout you? You okay?"

After her shocked reaction to Madden's attack, Cecily seemed to shake off the worst aftereffects by the time Will was released from the hospital. Over the weekend they'd both settled into something that resembled their usual routine. Finch bowed out of the baseball game, knowing that Phil Lees would gladly play Will's position as the team catcher. Over Saturday and Sunday, Will and Cecily were never more than ten feet from one another. Whenever she expressed any anxiety, he drew her into his arms until the moment passed. But he knew from his experience in Iraq that PTSD could take weeks to manifest. Sometimes years. J.R. provided a sorrowful example of how your life could unravel.

"I think so."

"You sure?" He glanced around the bog to see if any reporters were listening to him. When he saw no evidence of eavesdropping, he continued. "I mean, if you want to talk about it, like *really* talk about it, we can get some help."

"Yeah, I'm sure. You don't need to keep asking." Her voice perked up. "My baby's healthy. I love my job. I'm about to marry the man who saved my life. Why wouldn't I be all right?"

He laughed and then quickly stifled it under his breath. "You're right. And we're going to celebrate."

"We are?"

"Absolutely. Today's payday. I think I'm going to buy a new phone."

"Finally."

"And Saturday I'll take you back to Sausalito on the ferry."

"You want to try that again?" She sounded hesitant. "Could be bad luck, you know. What if you drop the phone overboard again?"

"No. I'm sure of it. And the weather's supposed to be clear. We can hang out on the stern deck."

"You're tempting fate, you know."

"No, no. It's exactly the opposite. Everything in my life is heading up. I want us to stay in this groove."

"I know. I want the same thing. Let's stay there and make it last forever."

He realized that her mood had changed. She sounded warm

and confident, and he felt the pleasure of being part of that.

"Forever and a day," he said. "All right, I've got to get back to work here. Love you."

"Love you too."

As he hung up, he chuckled to himself. At the illusion of forever. He believed that there was always — and only — one moment. One today. If you were lucky, another day followed. Then another. Soon the days marked a path through life. Sometimes, for those who realized it was possible, you could glimpse the possibilities ahead and chart a course. Maybe he and Cecily could do that without becoming rigid or obsessed. The mistake would be to blindly embrace the illusion that they were masters of their destiny. That alone could destroy them.

※

By four o'clock he'd finished the profile of Madden's criminal past and prison incarcerations. He was about to reread the story when his desk phone rang. The call screen showed an incoming line from Dixie Lindstrom.

"Will, I've got Agent Raymond Albescu on line two for you," Dixie said. "From the FBI."

The FBI. His pulse quickened. This call could go any one of a dozen different directions. He rubbed a hand over his face and realized that he should prepare. He opened a new file on his laptop.

"All right, Dixie," he said, "put him through."

"Press two and you'll be connected," she said and then added, "Good luck."

He pressed the flashing button — 2 — heard the line click, then leaned forward. "Agent Albescu. How can I help you?"

D. F. Bailey

"The question is, how can I help you?" Albescu's heavy whisper had an upbeat tone.

Finch typed a name on the top line of the screen: Albescu.

"I'm not sure what you're talking about."

"That's good." A soft laugh followed. "That means there's been no leaks."

"Uhhh ... what leaks are you referring to?" He typed: leaks?

"Vincent Sessions. We bagged him Saturday evening down in the Tenderloin." He paused as if he were considering how much to reveal on the phone. "He was going under an alias. Richard Babcock."

Finch typed the name and then paused. "How did you connect Babcock to Sessions?"

"I'd sooner do this in person. You want to hike over here to get the details?"

Will checked the time: 4:08. "I can be there by four-thirty."

"You better be. There's a press conference at six. You want your one-hour exclusive? It's either now or never."

Albescu hung up. Will held the phone in his hand, unsure how to move forward. After a moment he put the handset back in place. He scanned the surrounding pods where most of the reporters ticked silently at their keyboards. Olivia seemed preoccupied with a phone call. Costain had his face pressed against his computer screen — likely studying the details of another database search. At the desk behind Costain, Ross Sumner wrote notes on a yellow legal pad while he sipped coffee from a paper Starbucks cup.

Will closed the lid on his laptop and slipped it into his

courier bag. Then he tugged on his jacket and made his way to the reception desk to borrow the digital recorder from Dixie. On his way to the elevator bay, he laughed out loud, pumped a fist in the air, and reveled in the giddy feeling rising through his body.

※

It took twenty minutes for Will to reach the FBI field office. When the elevator doors slipped open on the thirteenth floor of the Phillip Burton Building, Agent Raymond Albescu stood alone, waiting for Finch. To his relief, there was no sign of Busby.

They squeezed through a large open area — the war room — filled with agents standing in groups of three or four. The room was abuzz with a taut, almost ravenous, energy. Next to the exterior windows, he spied Busby talking to two other agents. A smile creased Busby's face, and he laughed as if he were celebrating a victory.

"Don't mind the fuss," Albescu said as they walked beside the wall. "Sometimes the room temperature spikes when we bag a bad guy."

Albescu led Will to the same glassed-in meeting room where they'd interviewed him with Wally and Biscombe last week. He pulled a wide band of sheer drapes across the glass barrier to the door, and they sat facing one another at one end of the table. Will tugged his notepad from his courier bag and set the digital recorder between them.

"You mind if I record this?"

"Sure." Albescu laughed. "Usually it's the other way around."

"Right." Finch grinned to acknowledge the irony, clicked on the recorder and then wrote the date and time at the top of a page.

"Okay, let's dive in. Now, you said on the phone that the FBI captured Vincent Sessions in the Tenderloin on Saturday. That he was living under the alias of Richard Babcock, and that subsequently, he confessed to the serial killings we've been calling the five knives murders. Is that correct?"

"Yeah. He was picked up just after seven-thirty, Saturday night."

"And you've tied Sessions to a series of similar killings in Iraq that date back to 2005. How did you link the two?"

"Fingerprints. The crime techs used a new matching technique called a topology-based algorithm. Not as good as DNA, but close enough. The Army had a record of his prints which matched what we had from his kills in the US. And the icing on the cake? This morning Sessions made a complete confession in the presence of his lawyer."

A confession. Will studied Albescu for a moment. This meant that there'd be no reason to reveal J.R. as his source. Albescu grinned again; he understood the implications, too. "So this means that Felix Madden's murder of Seamus Henman had nothing to do with Vincent Sessions."

"Right. The five knives thing on Henman appears to be a copy-cat killing." Albescu tipped his head toward Will. "Just as you said."

Finch rested his pen across the wire spiral of the notepad and took a moment to piece this together. Part of him couldn't believe what he was hearing. "Let me make sure I've got this right. Vincent Sessions committed four murders in Iraq and more recently in Wichita and Reno. And you've got physical evidence *and* a confession to prove it."

"Yeah. Sometimes Christmas comes early." This time Albescu laughed with a lightness of spirit that revealed a persona different than the hard-nosed agent that he kept so tightly wrapped up. His long, weary face seemed fuller now. Even his voice carried an upbeat resonance.

"Frankly," he continued, "there're more killings than the two in Wichita and Reno."

"More?"

"At least six. From Miami on out."

"My God," he said. Just as Olivia had predicted. "Where else?"

He held up his right hand and counted off his thumb and fingers: "Miami, Atlanta, McComb — little town in Mississippi — then Nashville, Wichita, and Reno." He bunched his fingers in a fist to account for the sixth murder.

"So how'd you find him?"

"Textbook protocol." He shrugged as if it couldn't have been easier. "Once we got his mug shot from his Army file, we put out a BOLO."

"So what was it? An SFPD cop in a squad car spotted him?"

"No, two beat cops. And yes, the SFPD scored the takedown. In Paradise Coffee and Donuts on O'Farrell." Albescu nodded to acknowledge that the local boys in blue could sometimes pull their own weight. "When they spotted Sessions, they called for backup. Two cars arrived, and five minutes later

Sessions was cuffed and sitting in the back of a black-and-white. No resistance. No shots fired. Like I said, it was textbook."

"And the confession?"

"Busby and I were called in and started to grill him around eleven on Saturday night. He buttoned up until we provided a lawyer. We got him one a little after midnight. Then he slept on whatever advice and wisdom he received. Must've had a decent snooze, 'cause the next day he opened up. Frankly, I think he wanted to let it all go. You know, confess and lift the burden of guilt."

Finch glanced away. He wasn't so sure about the relief won through confession. As a teenager, he'd made weekly confessions to the Catholic priest and still felt the burden of his darkest thoughts. "So he told the whole story going back to Iraq?"

"Not yet. There's a helluva lot more to come, but he's copped to the six we've been tracking since Miami. Anyway, the Iraq killings are a done deal. We've got his prints, and the Army still have their cold casebooks open."

Will now had the full dimensions and scope of the story. Once he got to work, he'd be able to frame the article for Wally within ten minutes.

"I've got to tell you, Finch, without your tip, we'd still be blind on this thing."

Yeah?" Will suppressed a smile. "Was there a reward posted?"

"Sorry." Albescu turned his chin to one side, a gesture to indicate bad luck. "But you know, Busby was pressing for one. By the end of this week, the SAC would probably have given us the nod."

"Yeah? Who's that?"

"Anthony Rippin. He's going to be leading the press conference" — Albescu checked his watch — "in two minutes."

Finch made a final note: Anthony Rippin, Special Agent-in-Charge.

Someone knocked on the door and Albescu rose from his chair and pulled the curtain aside. Outside stood Busby. He tipped his head toward Finch. "Time," he mouthed through the glass and pushed his way back toward the middle of the room.

"You coming to the press con?" Albescu asked with a wry expression that suggested this was an inside joke amongst the agents. A jibe used to mock the press, the one — the only — public body that continually tested the limits and efficacy of the police and courts.

Finch considered the offer for a moment and realized that at best, his exclusive scoop would last no more than half an hour. Better to run down to a coffee shop, crank out his story as fast as possible and email it to Wally and Olivia.

"Thanks," he said. "I have to give it a miss. Maybe next time."

"Okay." Albescu held the door open as Finch dumped his notepad and the recorder into his bag. "I know you're fighting the clock."

While the media crews and reporters set up their cameras and settled in the chairs beneath the war room lectern, Finch made his way past the reception desk and over to the elevator bay. He stepped into an empty car. As the elevator dropped to the main floor, he closed his eyes and tried to absorb everything that had happened over the past week. Could it be? Had he outed two serial killers? More important, was he about to break the story that would make his career? Yes. Yes. And *yes.*

A minute later he stood on the sidewalk in front of the Burton Building. Half a block down the street he spotted a cafe. Philz Coffee. Perfect. He could set up his laptop and file the story from there. He jogged over to the corner of Larkin and Golden Gate.

"You've got this," he cried aloud and pumped his fist as he stepped into the crosswalk. He realized that the mass of pedestrians streaming towards him would think he was crazy. A madman. He didn't care. Let them believe whatever they wanted. Only one thing mattered now.

"Not only do you *have* this" — he lifted his arms in the air, and his voice rose in a screeching rant as he pressed through the crowd — *"you own it."*